"Are you always this impertinent?"

The soft, musical voice pulled Jack from his belief that no one could see him. He turned, and his gaze collided with the player from that morning. She was even younger than he'd thought, with an innocence that belied the fact coming to Chicago was probably the biggest thing that had happened to her.

Her jade eyes arrested him. They seemed to pierce through him, weigh him, and find him wanting. No woman ever did that.

Jack stood and found the girl was as petite as he thought. With creamy skin, red curls, and those green eyes, she looked like an Irish doll, one that barely reached his chest.

"Not really talkative, huh." She crossed her arms and stared at him. "I can't wait to see what you write in the paper. I'm sure each word will perfectly represent what is actually happening here."

"Slow down. Take a breath." He held up his hands. "I doubt you'll see the article, and I only write what I observe."

"A casual observer. Non-partial, no agenda at all." She jutted her chin out, stubbornness oozing from her.

"Claiming you haven't formed an opinion about me?" Jack flashed her his most charming smile. "I'm Jack Raymond."

"Katherine Miller. And yes, I already know what I need to about you."

An honors graduate of University of Nebraska-Lincoln and George Mason Law School, **CARA C. PUTMAN** is an attorney licensed in Virginia and Indiana. She's written six books for Heartsong Presents, including *Canteen Dreams*, a WWII historical set in Nebraska that won the ACFW 2008 Book of the Year for Short Historical. She currently has nine books out with three more releasing in 2010. Cara is also a wife, mom to three, home school teacher, occasional professor at Purdue, active church member, and all around crazy woman. (Crazy about God, her husband, and her kids, that is.) You can learn more about Cara at www.caraputman.com.

Books by Cara C. Putman

HEARTSONG PRESENTS

HP771—Canteen Dreams
HP799—Sandhill Dreams
HP819—Captive Dreams
HP856—A Promise Kept
HP876—A Promise Born

A Promise Forged

Cara C. Putman

Heartsong Presents

To my uncles Rick and Bruce Kilzer, both great baseball fans. And to my aunt Laurie Kilzer, who has always made me feel like an amazingly special person. My life has been so much richer because of you.

Much thanks to fellow author Cindy Thomson for ensuring I had the softball scenes right. A task since I'm a football lover! And to Scott Shuler, archivist at the Center for History in South Bend, Indiana, which houses the archives of the AAGPS/BL, for opening the archives to me and helping me navigate the wonderful files and resources the center has accumulated.

A note from the Author:
I love to hear from my readers! You may correspond with me by writing:

Cara C. Putman
Author Relations
PO Box 721
Uhrichsville, OH 44683

ISBN 978-1-60260-757-6

A PROMISE FORGED

Our mission is to publish and distribute inspirational products offering exceptional value and biblical encouragement to the masses.

PRINTED IN THE U.S.A.

one

May 1943

The taxi rolled to a stop, and Kat Miller wanted to pinch herself. Make sure she really sat outside the Chicago landmark. Wrigley Field. Women streamed through the gates in ones and twos, some swaggering but most staggering a bit as if starstruck by their location.

Wowzers.

When a man showed up at a softball game she played in a few months ago, she never dreamed it would lead to an invitation to play for the nascent All-American Girls Professional Softball League. She'd heard rumors of the forming league, but she hadn't dared to hope that someone would consider her or that her parents would give their blessing.

No, Kat was many things. But dreamer never topped the list. She had a strong head on her shoulders. Knew what to expect from life. This was not it.

"Calm down, Katherine Elizabeth Miller." She mimicked her mother's strong tone that talked her out of many a crazy phase. "Get out there and do what's needed. You received a letter, and you belong here as much as the next girl."

The driver looked at her through the rearview mirror. "You done talking to yourself? Ready to pay and get out of my cab?"

"More ready than you can imagine." Kat fished a bill from her pocket and handed it to the man. Grabbing her glove, she slid to the door and opened it. "Have a great day, mister."

"Yeah. You, too, kid." The man shook his head with a slight grin creasing his face.

She stepped out, and the cabbie peeled away, already intent

on his next fare. Kat stood rooted like concrete to the sidewalk, stomach churning at the thought she was this close to the home of baseball greats. Now that she stood closer, the others walked with shoulders back, heads high, ready to take the field and use her to clean it up. Why had she come all the way from Dayton on the basis of one letter?

Simple words. Yet words that had launched a dream she hadn't realized she'd harbored. *We invite you to the tryouts for the All-American Girls Professional Softball League.* The rest of the letter contained a list of details: When to show up. What to bring. What was at stake. The salary range if she landed a contract.

Her breath heaved in and out until she saw black spots. She wanted this. A chance to spend the summer traveling the region. And a team that would pay her to play a game she loved. She had to succeed this week at tryouts. She refused to go home with her head hanging.

Kat took a step toward the stadium.

Ready or not, she'd arrived.

Mom and Dad hadn't discouraged her, and she'd spied a shadow of pride on the face of her big brother, Mark. Get paid to play softball? Why wouldn't she try out? She'd loved the sport since the moment Mark had let her tag along to his games. Over time she'd badgered him enough to make him show her the basics. Hitting, bunting, throwing, catching, sliding, she did it all. Did it well enough that eventually Mark's team put her in when one of the guys didn't show.

Even Mom supported her, despite many of her mother's friends seeing the activity as less than feminine and downright questionable. What girl would choose to play in the dirt and bruise and batter her body in the pursuit of a small ball?

Someone jostled past Kat, bringing her back to the present. The uniforms the gals wore were as varied as the women. Some wore short skirts with leggings that made her long pants appear out of place. Others wore shorter pants, reminiscent of men's teams. Most wore their team jackets, the different hues creating a kaleidoscope of colors. As she walked through a turnstile at one of the gates and into the stands, Kat tried to absorb it all.

A woman with cropped curls, a baseball cap shoved on top, slammed into her. "Whatcha gawking at?"

Kat wrinkled her nose. Was that chew in the woman's mouth? Maybe it was a good thing her mother hadn't accompanied her after all. "Excuse me."

"Excuse yourself. See ya on the field. May the best one win." The gal grinned, revealing crooked teeth. "That would be me." She scampered down the stairs, not turning to see if Kat followed.

Father, help me. I want this. Oh, how she wanted this. If she was selected, maybe her friends would realize she really did excel at softball. That it wasn't merely a strange obsession to be tolerated with a grin. *But even more, Lord, I want to be Your light. Show me why You have me here.* Surely He had a reason.

As she stared at the more than two hundred assembled women, she prayed He did.

❧

Jack Raymond shook his head. Of all the harebrained schemes, this latest from Chicago Cubs owner Philip Wrigley took the cake.

All-American Girls Professional Softball League. Seemed like a misnomer of the worst kind. He'd always imagined himself covering baseball for a major newspaper, and here he was—in Chicago, granted—but covering. . .*girls*.

The cherry on top of the sundae proving the world had gone crazy.

How would this launch him from small-town Cherry Hill, Indiana, to the big leagues with a bona fide Chicago paper? He shook his head, disgust roiling his stomach. He could not imagine staying in Cherry Hill any longer than required. He'd love to have moved on yesterday. Somewhere he'd find the story that launched his career to a real paper with real articles about real sports.

This wasn't it.

Jack pulled his hat lower over his eyes and slouched in the bleacher. The handful of other reporters who'd showed up looked as ready to fall asleep out of sheer boredom as he did.

One snorted and roused from his nap long enough to shift in his seat.

Yep, this was the assignment to make him consider a career change. Maybe he should convince the draft board that, even though his knee had been destroyed in a college baseball game, he could soldier with the best of them.

Jack clamped his jaw. He hated acknowledging he couldn't do something. Even more, he hated *being told* he couldn't do something. Ha, he hated weakness of any kind.

Maybe that's why he despised the idea of covering weak women playing a sport designed for men. He only had to ignore the thousands of semiprofessional women's teams playing across the country. At least that's what his publisher told him, and since Ed Plunkett signed his checks, Jack had no choice. To an extent. He'd write the stories. But it didn't mean he had to turn into one of those hacks who said whatever the publisher wanted.

Wrigley and a few other men walked to the center of the playing field. Saved from his thoughts, Jack pulled his notebook from his jacket pocket. Maybe Wrigley had something newsworthy to say. Wrigley clapped his hands and beckoned the girls his way. It looked like a brood of hens flocking toward the thin man with his dapper fedora clamped tight on the top of his head. The women milled around. Many pushed close to the cluster of men, but a few hung around the edges, appearing uncertain. Jack leaned forward to scan the group.

"Ladies, welcome to Wrigley Field. You are competing for a limited number of slots in the All-American Girls

Professional Softball League. Show us the best you have. The evaluations begin now and will be rigorous. Each team has fifteen slots, so less than one third of you will find a spot on a team. And lest you think I overstate myself, the cuts begin tonight."

Jack heard a sharp intake of breath, and several of the women shuffled where they stood. Shoulders tightened, backs stiffened, and feet shifted. The tension hung thick over the diamond.

"Never forget you're here to show us women can play like men, while never letting us forget that you're women."

A lanky reporter next to Jack groaned. "Did he just say that?"

"Yep." Jack stuck out his hand. "Jack Raymond."

"Paul Barton, South Bend. Nice to meet ya." The guy shook his head. "I doubt these *ladies* can play."

"I don't know. I watched a kid play a couple of years ago in Ohio. I thought the team was crazy to have her out there—the only girl on a roster packed with guys. But you should have seen her." Jack shrugged. "She flew all over that diamond. I haven't seen many like her." That girl had almost made a believer of him, but he didn't expect that kind of magic here. Wouldn't it be something if she'd made the trip? The odds were too slim. These girls would play a little ball and head home without an impact. The league would implode within the year, and Wrigley would move on to his next crazy idea.

Another man leaned in. "You haven't watched the right women play. Some of them are amazing." He must have noticed Jack's skepticism. "Watch and see. I think you'll be surprised today. Rick Daley, down from Racine."

"Rick." Jack shook his hand then turned back to the diamond. The women listened in varying stages of attentiveness as the speeches continued.

"After practice tonight, you'll start charm school."

A murmur rose from the field, some of the women gesturing. Charm school? For softball players? This got better all the time.

Most of the gals looked like they only wanted to prove they could play. Charm was the last thing on their minds.

How could one pound around bases while running on tiptoes? The image made him chuckle. A girl switching between running and holding back so she could dance to home. Not what one normally equated with the game.

Jack looked down and stopped when one gal caught his eye as the sun bounced off her red curls. Based on the freckles dotting her face, she'd spent a fair amount of time outside. Must not play indoors on concrete rather than a grass field. She looked like a young kid, not old enough to have graduated from high school. A ball played easily through and around her fingers as she stood there. She looked at ease, then he noticed a slight tremor running up her back.

The kid had some kind of spunk even if her body betrayed her nervousness.

Her willowy form didn't have the size of some of the gals. The first time someone charged the plate she defended, she'd get knocked across town. Bet she played in the outfield somewhere.

She scanned the stands, connected with his gaze, and winked. A wide grin crossed her face as if she couldn't imagine standing anywhere else. He shook his head. A perfect demonstration of what was wrong with women in a sport. How could you maintain feminine decorum while sliding, throwing, and running around bases? Guess Wrigley thought charm school was the answer. A ripple flowed through him as he watched her.

Maybe joy bubbled from her for no other reason than that she stood there. Maybe the invitation to tryouts satisfied her.

No. She wouldn't be here without a deep desire. Only

someone filled with pep or a dream would make the effort to come to Chicago for tryouts. Only a few of the gals down there held contracts. The rest would practice, wait, and pray. There weren't many slots, so most would go home disappointed after their time in the Windy City.

He hoped to join them. Even returning to Cherry Hill, the small town where he'd been banished after an article riled a powerful reader, would be an improvement over covering a women's league. The town was fired up about having its own team. He didn't understand the city fathers' enthusiasm for the scheme, but they'd raised the necessary funds to join the other five inaugural cities. And his editor had sent him to cover try-outs and get the local community even more excited with stories about the players that would form the heart of the Cherry Hill Blossoms.

He could imagine the headlines now: SALLY SMUTHERS THRILLED TO LEAVE THE COWS AT HOME AND PLAY BALL ALL SUMMER.

Ugh.

Human-interest nonsense.

There certainly wouldn't be enough action happening for sports pieces. Unless they covered a column inch or two.

Watching the girls mill, Jack snorted. He'd watch and report. If they couldn't play, he wouldn't sugarcoat.

He pulled a pack of gum—Wrigley's of course, though its inferior Orbit brand—from his pocket and shoved a piece in his mouth. He chomped hard while watching the coaches run the girls through drills. A few looked like they knew what they were doing. They slid into base with no thought for the bruises that would form. Leaped for balls. Chased ground balls. Threw each other out. Pitchers wound up and threw underhanded pitches with a speed that made his arm ache.

After a couple of hours he couldn't watch another drill. Especially when a few of the players appeared more tentative and unsure of themselves as the day wore on.

"Leave it all on the diamond or go home. This isn't powder-puff baseball."

Paul slapped him on the shoulder. "You've got it. Some of these gals won't make it to tomorrow playing like that."

Jack grinned. "It's tough to powder your nose while running to home, isn't it?"

"I wouldn't know." Rick patted his cheek. "I've never needed the powder. Maybe some blush though."

They laughed, and Jack enjoyed the moment. Then he looked down. Caught the redhead staring at him, heat flowing from her gaze. The girl looked as mad as an editor with empty space on the front page.

She stomped closer. "Who gave you the right?"

"What?"

"Who gave you the right to make fun of us?"

"Miller, get back over here." A manager bellowed his command, bringing her steps to a halt. Jack jotted down her last name along with a note to track down her first. She might make a good subject for his first piece. Profile her movements through training camp.

She stared at him a moment longer then pivoted. "Yes, sir." She marched back to the drill, throwing a look over her shoulder at him, the breeze playing with her curls.

Rick shook his head and chuckled. "She got your number."

Paul nodded. "Let's see if she can play."

Jack settled back and watched. The girl moved through the drill as if fueled by her frustration. A fluidness to her movements reminded him of that kid from Ohio. What were the odds?

Nah.

But as he watched, he had to admit she played just like that kid. In fact, the way the ball played through her fingers like it was an extension of her made him certain it was the same girl. She was a dynamo on the field, and she wasn't the only one.

Some of the women played well. Quite well. So they might know a thing or two about the game.

Didn't mean people would pay to watch.

Without that, the league would flop before it launched.

two

The day's drills might have ended, but the lectures hadn't.

Sweat caked Kat's body after a day of hard practice. Some of the gals had collapsed on the ground, wrung out by the work. Kat tried to keep on her feet but longed for a soaking bath and large meal. Lots of fruit and meat. She hadn't been this hungry in a long time.

"If you are selected to join a team, you will dress, act, and carry yourself in a manner that befits the feminine ideal." Mr. Wrigley stood back in his spot near the pitcher's mound.

"Blimey. What's that mean?"

Kat glanced at the gal next to her. The girl's nose twitched as if she smelled something unbecoming.

"I don't know." The uncomfortable image of sliding into a plate in a skirt edged through Kat's mind. "I'm sure they have a plan. We'll find out when we're selected."

"Maybe I don't want to be selected."

"Sure you do. I wouldn't have made the trip from Dayton if I wasn't willing to do what it takes to play. Within reason, of course."

"That's just it." The gal shrugged. "We don't know if their 'within reason' matches ours. I'm Dolly Carey."

"Kat Miller." She scanned the women in front of her. "As long as they don't ask me to do anything immoral or indecent, I'm open to considering it."

"I suppose."

"Each evening after you clean up, you will head to the Helena Rubinstein Salon for lessons." Wrigley rubbed his hands together and bounced on his heels.

A salon?

"Your courses will include walking, sitting, speaking, clothing choices, applying makeup, and other skills essential to representing the best of the feminine ideal." Wrigley smiled at the girls.

"He ain't looked too closely at me, has he?" Dolly rolled her eyes. "I don't fit anyone's feminine ideal."

Kat looked the girl over. Short and stout, Dolly had a pretty smile and eyes that danced with glee. "Oh, I think you do."

"Tell that to my mother. She swears there's not a lick of femininity in me or I'd be at home, hunting for a husband, rather than standing here determined to play ball."

"My mom's glad I'm here rather than chasing a boy. I'm seventeen, an age she thinks is way too young." Kat laughed. She could imagine the look on the face of her big brother, Mark, if she marched home wearing a guy's ring. At least things hadn't gotten that serious with Bobby, a guy from her school. Besides, he didn't understand baseball. Any man who wanted to be interested in her had to like the things she did. "My family thinks I have to finish high school first." She rolled her eyes. "Like I'd do anything else."

Dolly looked away. "Wish I'd had that option."

"You didn't?"

"I needed to help at home. It happens when you're the oldest of ten."

Kat couldn't imagine not finishing school or having that many siblings. Even if she married young and started a family like her older sister, Josie, she wanted to learn all she could so she could be the best wife and mother possible to her family. There was too much out there she didn't know yet. And the thought of attending the University of Dayton where her father taught seemed like the logical next step after she finished her senior year of high school.

"Before you leave, we want to show you something." Mr. Wrigley's words pulled Kat from her thoughts. "This is the uniform the teams will wear."

A woman stepped onto the diamond. She twirled a bat over her shoulder and preened as she walked in front of the assembly. Kat's jaw dropped as she stared at the outfit. "We're supposed to play in that?"

That was a dress. No other word described it. A short skirt in an ugly shade of peach, with a top that buttoned to the side.

Dolly sucked in air through the gap in her front teeth. "It's awfully short. Can you imagine sliding into base?"

Kat shook her head, wincing at the image of the rash and bruise she'd get. A general murmur rose as the player up front continued to pirouette.

"That looks more like an ice-skating outfit than a softball uniform." Kat bit her tongue rather than say what she really thought. Only a fool would design something like that and think women could play ball in it.

"Enjoy charm school. You report there in an hour."

An hour? Kat groaned. So much for a soaking bath. She'd be lucky to get a shower and a meal.

Kat joined the flood of women headed to the hotel. She unlocked the door to her room and stumbled on a packet on the floor. She picked it up, back muscles protesting.

Charm school and dresses. Just wait till she wrote Mother a letter with those details. Maybe Mother's friends would approve when they heard what was required after practice. What did charm school have to do with softball? Kat collapsed on the bed, packet in hand, and closed her eyes. A nap sounded so good, but there wasn't time. Not if she wanted to clean up before dinner and charm school.

The scratch of a key in the door forced Kat to a sitting position. Nobody else should be in here. She scanned the room again. Nope, no unfamiliar luggage hidden against a wall or under furniture.

The door opened, and a suitcase pushed through, followed by a woman.

"Aren't you cute?" A stocky woman with crazy, curly hair

smiled at Kat as she wrestled the suitcase into the room. "Where are you from?"

"Dayton, Ohio." Kat smiled at her. "My name's Katherine Miller, but all my friends call me Kat."

"Well, Katherine 'Kat' Miller, I'm Lola Leoppold from southern Indiana." A soft twang peppered her words. "It's a pleasure."

Kat smiled. She might not have a room to herself, but Lola looked like the kind of person who'd make a good roommate. "What's your position?"

"Whatever will get me on a team." Lola hefted her case onto the second twin bed. "Wooh! Guess I packed too much. I'd think it contained rocks if I didn't know better. I've got to get away from home for a while, and the pay's good."

Fifty dollars a week or more. Great wages for a girl who hadn't finished high school. "It would be nice."

Lola snorted. "Doesn't look like you need the money."

Kat looked down at her sweaty outfit. She'd worn this uniform all last season, and it had lost its new shine awhile ago. If Lola thought this made Kat look like she was made of money, there wasn't much Kat could do to change that perception. A shiver traveled down her spine. Would everyone look at her so critically? Maybe she hadn't prepared for the cutthroat environment.

"What's in that envelope you're holding?"

Kat looked down at the packet. "I don't know. It was on the floor when I arrived."

"Aren't you curious?"

"Suppose I should be." She didn't open it. Instead Kat stared at it, imagining what it contained.

"You afraid it's a letter sending you home?" Lola snorted. "It's too early for that."

Maybe, but still. . . Kat took a deep breath and tore back the flap. She slipped out the sheets then scanned the first. "It's a handbook."

"See, nothing to get worked up about. Let me see it." Kat tossed the pamphlet to Lola, who opened it. "Here you go. 'Your mind and your body are interrelated, and you cannot neglect one without causing the other to suffer. A healthy mind and a healthy body are the true attributes of the all-American girl.'" Lola batted her eyes then laughed. "What a bunch of hooey."

"Regardless, this"—Kat waved a letter in the air—"says we need to be in the lobby in ten minutes for the walk to charm school."

"Then you'd better run through the shower fast, sister." Lola sniffed the air. "Or the charm will end before it begins."

Kat grabbed a change of clothes and hurried to the bathroom. With her rough edges, Lola might not be the person she would have picked for a roommate, but she'd certainly keep the training experience interesting.

After a quick shower, Kat dressed and headed downstairs to join the group walking to the charm school. Mother had always stressed manners and acting like a lady. What could Kat possibly learn?

❧

Jack slouched in a chair against the wall. He'd picked it because of the tall, fake palm tree tucked next to the seat. Maybe if he was really good and lucky, the evening would pass without many of the players noticing him.

That he sat in the Helena Rubinstein Salon was proof positive he needed to keep his mouth shut. The next time he thought something mildly entertaining, he'd keep it to himself, not give Ed the opportunity to send him to the wolves, er, salon.

This did not qualify as sports reporting any way he looked at it.

It might make the society page if he were unlucky. The best hope was that Ed came to his senses and realized what a horrible idea it was to give column inches to charm school.

A primly dressed young woman ushered the players into a large room. She glided across the room like a pro, while many of the players clomped into the ballroom. Jack covered a smile. The instructors had their work cut out for them if they planned to remake all these ladies in less than a week.

"Are you always this impertinent?"

The soft, musical voice pulled Jack from his belief that no one could see him. He turned, and his gaze collided with the player from that morning. She was even younger than he'd thought, with an innocence that belied the fact coming to Chicago was probably the biggest thing that had happened to her.

Her jade eyes arrested him. They seemed to pierce through him, weigh him, and find him wanting. No woman ever did that.

Jack stood and found the girl was as petite as he thought. With creamy skin, red curls, and those green eyes, she looked like an Irish doll, one that barely reached his chest.

"Not really talkative, huh." She crossed her arms and stared at him. "I can't wait to see what you write in the paper. I'm sure each word will perfectly represent what is actually happening here."

"Slow down. Take a breath." He held up his hands. "I doubt you'll see the article, and I only write what I observe."

"A casual observer. Non-partial, no agenda at all." She jutted her chin out, stubbornness oozing from her.

"Claiming you haven't formed an opinion about me?" Jack flashed her his most charming smile. "I'm Jack Raymond."

"Katherine Miller. And yes, I already know what I need to about you."

"Ladies, if you'll all find a chair." The older lady at the front of the room, Helena Rubinstein maybe, clapped her hands as other staff shooed the players to seats.

"Time's up."

Katherine stared at him another minute. "Guess you'll have

to prove me wrong later." She strolled to a vacant chair. The gals on either side highlighted her delicate beauty.

Jack chuckled and rubbed the back of his neck as he considered her words. He could think of a dozen ways to show her how her pulse could race in the presence of the right person. Katherine Miller was no different from the other women who succumbed to his charms.

The women stood to their feet, scraping hundreds of chairs across the floor. He shuddered and wondered how to escape the torture chamber.

About the time he didn't think he could watch one more person walk across the room or endure another player being told everything wrong with her appearance, the session ended. The women left the building, many rushing out the door, all decorum taught in the last hours abandoned. A few stayed in their chairs, talking in small groups.

Katherine sat by herself, stiff and unyielding. He wondered what bothered her.

Only one way to find out. Jack walked over to join his star. "Molded to the chair?"

She frowned at him. "What?"

"Most people flew out of here the moment they were free, but you're still here."

"I guess I am. Your powers of observation astound me, Mr. Raymond."

Point to the kid. "Jack. Call me Jack."

"Maybe." She grinned at him, a cute dimple appearing in her chin. "Are you hungry?"

"Sure. What did you have in mind?"

"A huge slab of pie."

He could imagine she was hungry after the day of exercise, but as her gaze flitted about the room, something more underlined her request. "Let's find you something to eat. Can't have you melting away."

One of the chaperones stood at the door watching the

women leave. When Katherine saw her, she groaned. "I guess we'd better forget the pie."

"Why's that?"

"Rule number three. All social engagements must be approved by a chaperone. I can't give them any reason to think I won't make a good player or follow their silly rules." She chewed a fingernail, and her shoulders sloped, all hints of perfect posture from minutes ago displaced.

Watching her he wanted to do something to take her mind off whatever had her tense. "Let me walk you back." At least then he could try to entertain her.

A shy smile teased her lips. "I think that works in the rules."

As they walked, he told her stories about different events he'd covered. He did his best to make every city hall meeting sound exciting or ridiculous. Ridiculous wasn't too hard when he mentioned the feud about somebody's goat eating the neighbor's prize roses. Her laugh surrounded him, and the tension eased from her body.

They reached the door of the hotel, and she turned to him. "Thank you."

"For what?"

"Helping me forget that I could be cut tonight." Her dimple reappeared for a fleeting moment. "Good night." She slipped through the rotating door and disappeared into the lobby.

She might make this week interesting after all. He'd make certain of that.

three

The next morning Kat stalked to Wrigley Field. Her body ached, each movement emphasizing the nonstop activity of the day before. It didn't matter. Kat would leave everything on the diamond. No way would she be sent home without knowing she had done all she could to prove she could play.

Pandemonium reigned as the managers organized the girls into groups. Kat glanced into the stands and found Jack. This time he looked bored out of his mind as he slouched on the bleacher. A pad of paper sat next to him, pages fluttering in the wind, but a pen remained tucked behind his ear. He couldn't write a story if it stayed there. Jack caught her watching him and winked. Heat climbed her neck, reaching her cheeks. She longed for a tan that would cover the color.

He leaned forward and motioned for her.

Kat sneaked a look at the coach and sidled toward the bleachers. "Yes?"

"Just wanted you to know you're an even better player now than you were the first time I saw you play."

"The first time? Yesterday?" What was the man talking about?

"No, several years ago I got to watch you back in Ohio. The only girl on a team of men."

"That's what I'm used to."

"Not after this week." He leaned back again, taking on a bored air. "You'll be busy playing with the gals after this week."

She wanted to believe he was right. But. . .too much could still go wrong. And too many other women here were too good at softball.

"Miller."

Kat startled as her name was barked. "Yes, sir?"

"You here to play or watch the reporters?" A burly manager frowned and pointed back to the diamond.

"Here to play, sir."

"Then get in line with the rest of 'em. This is worse than herding cats."

Kat laughed at the image. She could just see the man trying to organize her tabby and calico along with another three hundred or so cats. A project destined for failure.

She gave the manager her full attention and soon fielded balls along with the rest in her group. Her field of vision narrowed until the white balls were all she could see. She anticipated where they'd roll and flew around her area, determined to catch each one.

The next time she caught her breath and looked in the stands, Jack had disappeared.

Her heart sank. She shook off the sensation. Why should she care if he sat there or not? Reporters didn't understand softball anyway. When had one ever gotten the story right? No, in her experience, reporters undervalued any sport girls played. Why submit to more of that?

She didn't need anyone to tell her she played well. Especially not a reporter who couldn't play the game if his survival depended on it.

The morning passed in a blur of running, sliding, catching, and throwing. By the time lunch was served, Kat felt like she'd done everything she could on the diamond. Already she felt her muscles tightening. If she didn't stretch, she'd stiffen too much to play in the afternoon. Kat gulped water as she sat at a table with Dolly and other exhausted players. Subdued conversation flowed as they ate and introduced themselves.

Some had journeyed from as far as Canada and Florida. The common consensus was that each of them had to make a team. The options back home didn't satisfy any of them.

Kat looked around and noticed several people who hadn't made appearances. "Where is everybody?"

"Didn't you hear?" Dolly groaned. "Some got calls last night. They were sent home. Already. They really made cuts after the first day."

Kat gulped. "Cut? Already?"

"Yep." Dolly shivered. "Can you imagine? They must be serious about finding the best players. And quickly!"

That settled it. Kat would play so hard she couldn't move if that's what the managers expected. Guess it would prepare her for what she would face if she made a team.

No. Not if. *When* she made a team.

❧

Jack rubbed his head then slapped his hat back on. The sun pounded down, and he wished for a bit of shade. What he wouldn't give for a desk back in the newsroom. The comfortable chaos sounded wonderful compared to the boredom of watching yet another day of drills. Spring training only accentuated his inability to play the game he had loved.

A breeze ruffled the newspaper on the bleacher next to him. He'd hunted and found a copy of this morning's *Cherry Hill Gazette*, all for the spunky redhead. He couldn't wait to toss her the issue and watch her reaction. There would be one. He had no doubt of that. Whatever it was, he'd wager it would entertain.

The managers ran the women through more drills. Jack winced each time he watched a gal throw herself into a slide toward home plate. He could only imagine the bruises forming under their shorts and pants. Nothing compared to what would happen once they wore those ridiculous uniforms Wrigley's wife had designed.

He enjoyed sports as much as the next person, but the intensity on the field was mind-boggling. A couple of women almost came to fisticuffs over catching a ball.

Jack shook his head and waited for the practice to end.

Fortunately he didn't have to cover charm school tonight. The images from last night still haunted him. Each gal had been evaluated, sometimes brutally. What had started as entertainment left him feeling bad for some of them. They couldn't control what God had given them to work with. Tell that to the salon staff who took it as a personal affront.

Yet another reason to be glad God made him a man. No one cared if his hair was thick, thin, or spotty. His eyebrows remained untouched, and thank goodness he didn't get told what cosmetics to use and where.

A shudder coursed through him at the thought.

This was supposed to be about softball. If last night was a realistic reflection, "powder-puff" accurately described the nascent league.

"All right. You're done, ladies. I'll see you in the morning." One of the managers dismissed the gals. "And don't forget your schooling tonight."

Groans rose from the crowd. Many turned and shuffled out of the park. A few collapsed on the field. Jack scanned the group for one with hard-to-miss auburn hair. He'd watched her off and on, and now when he wanted to talk to her, it figured he couldn't find her.

There.

He leaped to his feet and bounded down the last few steps, ensuring his path intersected with hers. "Hey, kid."

She stopped, the weary slump of her shoulders making him wonder if he should leave her alone. "Yes?"

"Thought you might like to see the article I wrote." He tossed the paper at her, and she caught it with sure hands.

"Thanks." Katherine flicked the paper at him in a wave and resumed her march to the exit.

He crossed his arms, waiting to see how far she'd go. "Aren't you going to read it?"

"What? You afraid no one will notice your name in print unless you force them to read it?" Her sharp words seemed to surprise her. She took a step back and exhaled. "I'm sorry. I'm not usually so. . .snippy. Forgive me?"

What did one say to that? "Sure."

"Thanks." A faint smile etched her drawn face. "I promise to read it if I can before heading to school." She sniffed the air playfully. "I think they'd appreciate it if I cleaned up first."

Jack decided to play along. "I wondered where that aroma started."

"Yours truly. Good night, sir."

"Good night." He should let her go on her way. Practice had ended, and he was free as a bird. Draft tomorrow's story, and then he could see some of Chicago. If he followed her, he'd end up at the salon, watching instructors teach the fundamentals of feminine sitting. What was so hard about it? Cross your legs and smile. Seemed straightforward.

But he found himself following then catching the beautiful Katherine Miller. The lingering thought of Polly, the girl he'd seen a few times in Cherry Hill, teased his mind. She wouldn't be thrilled to learn he'd spent time with another woman, but surely she'd agree Katherine was too young for him. He'd been out of college a couple years, and Katherine hadn't graduated from high school.

He almost believed those words himself. Almost.

"Want some company?"

Her steps slowed down, and she turned to him. "Mr. Raymond, are you always this incorrigible?"

"Mighty big word for a sixteen-year-old."

She pulled herself to her full height—maybe all five feet two inches. "I'm seventeen, for your information, and well educated."

He stopped short at her words then burst into laughter. "You are something."

"My brother agrees."

He leaned in to catch her mumbled words. "If you don't mind, I'm really too tired to banter." She rolled her neck. "I pray I don't get a phone call."

Jack frowned. What was she talking about? "Pardon?"

"You know. A call from the manager."

"Telling you what?"

She rolled her eyes like he didn't have a clue. "The one telling me to catch the next train home. That I'm wasting everybody's time and don't need to come back in the morning." Her words rushed faster and faster out of her mouth until they practically came out as one long word. Sweat dotted her forehead and upper lip.

"Look kid, you don't have to worry about that. You were all over the field again today. You play as well as any woman out there."

She closed her eyes and seemed to drink in his words. "I hope you're right." Smile lines creased around her eyes. "The good news is, God knows what I'm supposed to do next. I hope that includes playing softball here, but if not, He has something else for me."

"You seem pretty confident." Oddly so for someone so young.

"Absolutely. Some things never change, and God's promises are one of them."

❧

Despite her words Kat felt the strain of the day's drills as she bantered with Jack. Instead of resting in her room she joined the others back in charm school. Kat grabbed a seat with Lola and Dolly on either side.

Even after their conversation on the walk to the hotel, Jack had waited for her outside the hotel when she left for the walk to charm school. The man was relentless. "Any comments about your day?"

"Other than it was filled with drills? No."

"Come on. Just a sentence or two." He turned puppy dog eyes on her, and her heart flopped.

"I'm sorry." She'd stammered, trying to get her tongue to

cooperate as she drowned in his gaze.

"Just a word."

She shook her head.

A slow grin had transformed his face. "Don't tell me."

"Tell you what?"

"I stop your heart, make your pulse race."

She snorted. "Those are mutually exclusive."

He shrugged. "Your point?"

Kat stammered before sliding away. That insufferable man. Who did he think he was to insinuate he affected her? With a look or a word? Nobody did that.

She took a deep breath and then eased it out. Repeated. And she would repeat it over and over until her heart got the message and slowed its dramatic gallop.

Dolly leaned against her shoulder. "Are you okay?"

A chaperone glanced their way and frowned. Kat nodded but didn't answer. Suddenly she wasn't in the mood for anyone to tell her how to sit or stand. She didn't need instructions on how to make conversation with strangers.

Unless it was with that aggravating Jack. Maybe he needed tonight's lesson.

What she longed for was a long soak in a bubble-filled bathtub, dim lights, and a tall glass of Coca-Cola. Add a huge sandwich and platter of fruit, and she'd be a happy girl. Sounded like the perfect antidote to the long day and the stress of wondering if she'd made enough of an impression to stay through another day of camp.

Instead she stood and glided across the room with a book on her head—a book!—time after time after time. If she didn't know how to glide versus march by this time, she doubted a book and repetition would make a difference. Finally the taskmasters released them after three hours of walking, standing, and sitting.

That reporter hadn't stopped watching her the whole time. In a room filled with women, many more beautiful than she ever hoped to be, why focus his attention on her? It was enough to drive her to distraction.

❧

Each morning that week Jack strolled to Wrigley Field, wondering who would be left. Each day the field of prospective players shrunk, but the one he had his eye on remained. The shadows under her eyes darkened until he wondered if she bothered to sleep.

The morning of May 26 dawned. This was the day the remaining girls would find out who had made it. Who would fill the rosters for the six teams.

When he arrived at the park, the women were gathered around home plate. All gazes were focused on a blank easel that had been propped up near the pitcher's mound.

"Morning, Paul, Rick." Jack sidled past them onto the bench. "What are they waiting for?"

"Nothing's been posted yet." Paul leaned back with his arms crossed on his chest.

"It's one nervous group." Rick jotted a note. "The conversation keeps falling off, and you'll see every nervous habit known to man—er, woman, exhibited out there."

"So this is it. The new teams." Jack grinned. "I bet I know one of the members."

Rick guffawed. "We all know who that is. A certain redhead."

"You don't think she's qualified?"

Rick put his hands up in front of him. "I didn't say that. There's a bunch of women out there who are qualified but still won't have a slot at the end of the day. Most of them are."

True words. These women could play when they weren't checking their makeup or teeth.

Regardless, right now each one looked as nervous as a cub reporter in a newsroom full of Pulitzer Prize winners. Katherine stood at the edge of the crowd. The two next to her chattered like their mouths didn't have an off switch, but she chewed at a nail and waited. She held her body at stiff angles.

A man walked out onto the field with two sheets of paper. It felt as if all the oxygen disappeared from the area as the women waited for him to post the information.

"Glad I'm not them right now." Paul pulled out his skinny notebook and scribbled in it.

Jack nodded. His gaze kept returning to Katherine Miller. What explained this attraction? Did it stem from that one game years ago that he had watched her play? He remained unconvinced there should be a professional league for women. But there was no doubt she'd earned the right to play in it.

The man stepped back from the board, and a flood of women approached. They pushed and shoved in an attempt to get close. A woman ran her finger along the list then screamed in delight. Another walked away, shoulders hunched and head down. By threes and fours they reached the list and shrieked or cried. Some hugged each other, while others stood in shock. Most whose names weren't on the list slunk away, alone.

Katherine, however, remained to the side. Did she have any fingernails left? Why not push into the fray and discover if she'd made a team? The group got smaller until there was no reason she hadn't moved to the list. Unless she couldn't bring herself to check.

Poor kid.

Her nerves probably couldn't stand the suspense of not knowing or wouldn't allow her to propel her feet to the board so she could check.

This he could do something about.

"Catch you gents later." Jack stood and made his way to the aisle. He hopped the short wall at the edge of the bleachers and strode to Katherine.

The barest shadow of a smile graced her face when she saw him. He wanted to take her hand and rub the jagged edges of her nails. Tell her whatever the result, she was a great player in his book. Instead he shoved his hands in his pockets.

"Ready to find out if you made the team?"

She shook her head. "I can't do it."

"The fireball who threw herself all over this field all week to prove she'd earned a spot can't find the courage to read the board."

A momentary fire flashed in her eyes before she shook her head.

"May I?"

"I don't know. . . ."

"The answer won't change if I'm the one looking."

"Go ahead. And thank you."

Jack sauntered up to the board as if he didn't have a care in the world. In his opinion she'd make a great Rockford Peach or Kenosha Comet. Yep, as long as she was far from him, she'd make a great addition to any team. He didn't need the headache of following her career, not with this strange way he couldn't stop thinking about her. Imagine explaining that to Polly. Adorable, sweet Polly Reese who looked like a grown-up Shirley Temple and liked to spend her free time with him. Didn't hurt that his press pass gave them access to lots of places and events.

Katherine cleared her throat.

He jerked his thoughts back to the moment. "Sorry."

Jack ran his finger down the list. It was in alphabetical order, but he wanted to make sure he didn't miss her.

"Let's see: Anderson, Andrews, Bartholemew. . ."

"Oh, please."

"All right, all right. I won't read the list." He chuckled. "You could do this yourself, you know." He looked at her, noticed how pale she was. "Let's see, where was I?"

She pushed past him. "Enough. Grange, Jackson, Lyle, Miller. Katherine Miller." She sagged as if her muscles collapsed from relief. He put a hand under her elbow to support her. The surge of electricity that shot up his arm forced him to step back.

"Congrats, kid. What team are you on?" *Far away. Far away. Far away.* He silently chanted the words.

Her grin split her face. "Looks like I'm a Cherry Hill Blossom."

four

I'm a Cherry Hill Blossom. Thank You, Lord. Kat wanted to yell the words to the world. Instead she spun around and hugged Jack.

"Oh, I'm sorry." She tried to step back but found his arms wrapped around her. Tight. And it didn't feel so bad. In fact she might like his embrace if she let herself. What had gotten into her? She pushed against his solid chest.

"Congratulations, kid." His words were right, but as she looked up into his face, it looked pasty. Like he'd eaten something bad.

"Are you okay?"

He released her as if she'd become a hot potato and stepped back, tucking his hands firmly in his pant pockets. "Sure. Congrats. I'll see you around."

The insufferable man spun on his heel and disappeared before she could say anything. A tremble coursed through her. Fatigue? Adrenaline? The feel of his arms around her?

She didn't have time for this. The train transporting her to her new team left in a few hours. She needed to return to the hotel and pack her belongings. Place a call home to share the wonderful news.

But first, she had to see who else made the team. She scoured the list, smiling when she noticed Dolly had made the Racine Belles team and Lola would join her as a Blossom. She'd welcome the familiar face.

Soon she'd be transported to her new home away from home.

When she reached the lobby of the hotel, Kat passed groups of players. She stopped to hug a few who'd packed and were on their way home. Why had she been selected while others who played as well got sent home? She didn't know, but the sense of celebration stayed with her.

She slipped into the phone booth in the lobby. With trembling fingers she asked the operator to connect her with her parents' home. It took forever for the call to connect, and with each click she expected to hear a dial tone. Finally a ring.

"Hello, this is the Millers' residence."

"Mom?" Tears coursed down Kat's cheeks.

"Kat, are you okay?" An edge of worry tinged her mother's voice.

"Great, actually." Kat took a deep breath and swiped her cheeks. "I made a team."

"Honey!" Her mother squealed. "That's wonderful news! I wish your father or Mark were here so you could tell them. Which team?"

"I'm a Cherry Hill Blossom."

"That's close to Chicago, isn't it?"

"Yes. We'll be on the circuit playing the other teams."

"Can you come home before you go to Cherry Hill?"

"No." Kat looked at her watch, and her pulse jumped. "In fact, our train leaves for Cherry Hill in a couple of hours. I've got a lot to do before then." She hugged the phone against her ear. "I had to let you know before I got swept away." If only softball were the only reason she felt breathless. She'd have to slug that reporter the next time she saw him.

"Please let us know your playing schedule. Then we can plan to come to a game or two."

A lump formed in Kat's throat. How could she already miss her family so much? "I'd love that. And I'll let you know as soon as I know game dates."

"I love you, honey. Know we'll be praying for you. Stay close to God no matter how crazy your schedule gets."

"Yes ma'am." Kat wanted to tell her mom she'd done that all week but couldn't. She'd let the crazy schedule and fatigue interfere with her prayer and study time. She wouldn't let that continue. She'd need God to walk with her through whatever the next days and weeks brought. "Love you."

She hung up then leaned against the phone. An emptiness settled over the excitement. Here nobody knew her. She'd never felt so alone.

A fist pounded the phone booth. "Let someone else have a turn."

Kat jolted then slid back the door. "Sorry."

She tucked her chin and hurried to her room. If she didn't hurry, she'd get left. As she packed, she came across the paper that Jack had thrust at her days before. In the rush of practice and charm school she hadn't made time to read it. Pulling it out she flipped until she found an article he'd marked. Yep, his name sat on the byline.

A rather short article, it didn't take long to read. But she stopped when she saw her name.

Katherine "Kat" Miller is a great example of the women who have traveled to try out for the teams. A fireball at barely seventeen, she flies all over the field then stops to powder her nose.

What! She'd never done that. Well, other than that one time.

Quite subtly these women are told how to look good for a man at charm school. Not so subtly they are told how to whack the stuffing out of a ball, bump some chumpeine *on her derriere should said player block a base, and other fine points to technique. All in a day's work as they look for a good man after playing all day.*

Look good for a man? Powder her nose? Is that what he thought she was here to do? Play ball until she could ensnare a man? She balled up the paper and threw it across the room, where it bounced into the trash can. Insufferable man.

Why did his words sting?

❧

Jack threw his things in a satchel and zipped the bag. He needed to get a grip. The fact one little girl had made the Cherry Hill team should not catapult him into a tailspin.

What did it matter to him? After all, she'd be in town a few months and then go back to wherever she'd come from. Too bad his editor wanted him to follow one of the new team members and the manager had suggested her. He must have noticed the way the two had connected. Wait until Katherine learned of the assignment. He could see her response now. Either she'd launch into his arms or slap him. Either would be deserved. And neither sounded good.

A short taxi ride later Jack climbed out at Union Station. The train ride would give him the time he needed to polish the next article, as well as finesse a few special interest pieces. Ed was determined to launch the team in style. Might have something to do with the money he'd invested in the idea.

Jack wove through the maze of people, past the canteen packed with servicemen and servicewomen and finally worked his way to the tracks. His train puffed as it strained at the brakes. Jack broke into a run. He couldn't miss it. The next one wasn't until the following morning, and he'd never hear the end of it from Ed if he didn't get those stories turned in, along with an in-person account of training camp.

The sheer number of military uniforms present made Jack nervous. He didn't want to get bumped. The thought of sleeping in his bed sounded wonderful. But first he had to get on the train, find a seat, and file a story.

High-pitched laughter caught his attention. Jack froze. Surely the Blossoms wouldn't be on his train. Not tonight.

Jack turned slowly, hoped it looked casual and unrushed. There they were. Fifteen women and their chaperone, giggling like they'd won the biggest prize of their lives.

Katherine caught his eye and stonewalled him. A hard edge came over her face, and then she averted her gaze. What was that all about? She shifted her suitcase to her other hand and hurried past him to catch up with another gal, a gal who had the leggy look made so popular by Marlene Dietrich. She also had an air of experience that contrasted with Katherine's innocence. Jack had a bad feeling watching the two.

The conductor leaned out the last car. "All aboard."

The team picked up their pace, shuffling toward the car with cases banging against their already battered legs.

Jack hefted his satchel and hurried to join them. He should act the gentleman, help with the luggage. At least the cases he could. Before he could reach them, a porter sauntered up and started tagging the bags.

"I'll see that your bags reach Cherry Hill along with you." The porter grinned at the ladies and accepted the tips they pressed in his hands. He turned to Jack. "Help you with your bag, sir?"

"No, I've got it." He'd shove it in the rack above his seat or between his legs. It was small, and keeping it ensured he could get out of the depot quickly once in Cherry Hill.

Katherine watched him from the side. "You needn't be so abrupt. He only did his job."

Jack considered her, hearing the ring of truth in her words as well as the heaviness of fatigue. "You're right. Looks like he's burdened enough with your bags. I'm only trying to make his life easier."

She eyed the stack of bags. "I hope he gets them on in time." She rubbed a shoulder. "That's all I have for the summer. There's no time to go home, and who knows when I'll have time to shop."

"Isn't that what women do?" Jack grinned at her, trying to tease a response from her. "Shop at the drop of a hat?"

"We're in the middle of a war, Jack. It's tricky to find things I like."

"Kat Miller, plan to join us?" The chaperone stood in the doorway to the car, a frown engraved on her face. The woman had pulled her hair back in a bun that rested at the nape of her neck under a prim hat. Her suit was conservative and fit the look for a woman tasked with keeping those entrusted to her in compliance with the myriad rules the league had established.

"Yes ma'am. Good-bye, Jack." She followed the woman onto the car.

Jack watched a moment then turned and went the opposite direction, looking for a seat on another car. He needed as much distance as he could find between himself and the enchanting Miss Miller.

Once he found a seat and settled his bag overhead, Jack pulled out his notebook and went to work.

There's a powder-puff plot under way to take over the smelly old game of baseball. What once was the standard image of baseball—the tobacco-chewing, rough-around-the-edges, paunchy baseball player—is being replaced in towns like Cherry Hill with the reality of women who've attended charm school and training camp.

No one better represents this new group than young Katherine "Kat" Miller. A teenager from Dayton, Ohio, Kat played ball with her brother and other boys on teams around the city. Now she's a member of the Cherry Hill Blossoms.

A whiz on the diamond, Kat's pretty enough for a role in the movies. Feisty and dramatic, she has a flair for the game and hits a zone that makes balls fear her.

He smiled as he reread the beginning. Yeah, this was the stuff Ed wanted. Too bad it was so syrupy it made him sick.

❧

"Lookie here. It's the new darling of Cherry Hill."

Kat roused from her hotel bed, waves of exhaustion washing over her. The train had been delayed time and again in the short trip to Cherry Hill as military transport trains sidelined theirs. When they finally arrived in town around 2:00 a.m., she'd collapsed in the nearest bed.

She rubbed her eyes. "What time is it?"

"Time to read the paper." Lola tossed a crinkled section on her bed. "Don't let it go to your head. He's obviously got a crush on you."

"Who?"

"That reporter you talked to last night. Jack what's-his-name." Lola sat on the edge of Kat's bed and picked at the edges of her red fingernail polish. "Looks like he's decided to make you a star."

A star? What was the woman talking about? Especially after the things he'd said in the article he'd given her. Snagging a man indeed. "I doubt that."

She scanned the article, grimacing at the photo. She'd hated every moment of having her photo taken. The photographer had insisted she be in her uniform but checking her makeup in a mirror. Why couldn't he snap a photo during practice? No wonder they called it "powder-puff." An image the reporters had created. She was sick of that phrase, and it had only been a week.

As she reread the article, she slowed. Whiz on the field? Feisty and dramatic? With each word her heart pounded faster and heat climbed her cheeks.

"See what I mean?" Lola grinned, but a hard edge filled her gaze. "He's in love."

"I highly doubt that. He's too old for me. Why, he's twenty-five, and I'm not interested. I'm here to play softball, not get a boyfriend." Besides Bobby back home seemed to think they should spend their senior year together. Though she didn't think they were that serious.

"Sure. Well, if you get your privileged body out of bed, we have breakfast and meetings. Oh, and something called practice."

Lola disappeared out the door. What had Kat done to her? Maybe they wouldn't make good roommates, after all. For a moment, she wished Dolly had made the Blossoms instead of Lola. Oh well, there was nothing she could do about that.

Kat pulled on her robe then dug through her bag for her Bible. She'd need to find a church for those rare Sundays she was in town. Maybe her host family would let her join them. Regardless, she refused to start the day without first reading a psalm and praying. If the last week was any indication, she'd need all the fortification she could get to survive. But she wanted to do much more.

God had her here for a reason, and she wanted to be prepared. The only way to do that was to stay in communication with Him and make sure she fed her heart on a daily basis.

Be ready in season and out of season. She might not know exactly when He would call on her to represent Him, but she'd better prepare now.

Once she finished reading and praying, Kat got ready and hurried to the lobby.

"Everyone's eating at the diner next door." Faye Donahue sat in a stuffed chair, leg bouncing at a frenetic pace. "You're the last one, sister. Let's move before all the food's gone."

"I didn't realize anyone waited for me."

"Our chaperone says we have to stick together."

Kat swallowed hard around the sudden lump in her throat. This was not the way to make a good impression on the incredible pitcher. "I'm sorry."

"Don't worry about it. Let's move now. I'm starved."

Kat's stomach rumbled in answer. "I guess I am, too."

"They've got a busy day for us. Practice. Meet the local supporters. Meet our host families. Practice. Prepare for our first road trip."

Road trip. That made it all real. Ready or not, she'd play her first game in only a couple nights. The thought made her chest tighten. She could hardly catch a breath.

"Are you okay, kid?"

"Yeah. Pinch me, okay?"

Faye leaned over and gave her a good squeeze.

Kat jumped back. "Ouch. Guess I'm really here."

Now she had to prove to herself and the community she'd earned her spot and wasn't merely a pretty powder puff.

five

"Let's go see this team you've written so much about." Ed Plunkett slapped a battered felt hat on his head and tugged up his suspenders. Excitement reverberated from the guy as he rubbed his hands together.

Acid bubbled in Jack's stomach. "Sir, they might not be what you expect."

"Sure they will be. Angels who play like the boys. What's not to like?"

Plunkett had ordered all the staff to take their lunch break at the diamond. Memorial Field didn't hold any of the prestige of Wrigley Field, but it served the small city well. Blocks off Main Street, it usually hosted a constant run of Little League and community baseball games. This summer the Blossoms would dominate. All other games would be worked in around their aggressive schedule.

Just looking at the unending run of games made Jack tired, and he didn't have to play them. Once the season kicked off, the girls would play eight games most weeks. When they'd eat and sleep remained a mystery, especially when they traveled to away games.

"Come on, come on. No time to waste, girls and boys." Plunkett shooed the handful of reporters, salesmen, and secretaries out the door. Jack hurried to keep up, ignoring the hitch in his steps. Lousy day for his knee to act up.

By the time they reached the field, Jack tried to hide the way he huffed. Plunkett had powered up the street as if Rommel and his troops lurked behind. Jack pulled his handkerchief from his pocket and swiped his forehead. When he looked up, he froze. The townspeople had filled the bleachers.

It might be a routine practice to the players, but to the town it was the birth of their team.

Lunch boxes sat open, the contents consumed almost as an afterthought as everyone focused on the fifteen women on the field.

The team had dressed in practice clothes so did not have their fancy-schmancy dresses on. He couldn't wait to see the fans' reaction to those silly concoctions. The manager could field a team of nine, so practice looked lopsided. Katherine Miller hovered in the shortstop area, intent on the ball. The kid concentrated like nobody's business when on the field.

Faye Donahue wound up on the pitcher's mound, her underhanded pitch hurtling toward the batter. Jackie Smarts held her stance and popped the ball at the perfect moment to send it hurtling through the air, right into Katherine's glove.

"Did you see that!" Plunkett pumped his fist in the air. "Mark my words, boys, this was what the town needed. The Blossoms will put us on the map. Give the factory workers something worthwhile to do in the evenings after their shift. Woo-whee!"

"Sure you don't want to write the articles, sir? Your enthusiasm would be a great addition to them." Jack crossed his fingers. Maybe he'd get to do real stories on real topics. . .like rubber drives. What was he thinking? This assignment was the best thing that had happened to him.

Plunkett frowned at him, lines creasing the man's balding dome. "Raymond." The growl caused Jack to perfect his posture. "You will cover this team, and you will do a good job. Or you can hunt for a job on some other paper. Good luck with that in these times."

"Yes, sir. I mean, no, sir. I love writing about the powder puffs."

Plunkett rolled his eyes. "I'm going to watch my team play. In peace. I suggest you look for your next story. You'll find plenty on that diamond."

Jack inched away from Plunkett, all too glad to avoid the man's attention for a while. When would he learn to keep his big yap shut? His dad had always warned him that a fool made his identity clear every time he opened his mouth. He'd sure done enough of that lately.

Did he want to report or not? If he did, then he needed to buckle down and focus. His pride would kill his career before he established it if he didn't guard his thoughts.

He wanted to do a good job. So why couldn't he focus where he needed? His dreams of bigger things would never happen if he didn't do what was required here.

The crowd jumped to its feet with a roar.

Jack stood and searched the field. What just happened?

Ah. Katherine took a quick bow in center field. Her eyes sparkled, and her cheeks flushed. The girl was stunning and having the time of her life. She waved then handed the ball to Faye. With a blown kiss and last wave, she hurried back to her spot and regained her focus.

❧

Concentrate. The roar as the crowd jumped to its feet rang in her ears. Kat hadn't expected the enthusiasm for a simple practice to be so complete.

"Ready to play rather than be a prima donna?" Lola's words rasped with a hard edge. Standing at second base, the woman seemed even more competitive in the twenty-four hours they'd been in Cherry Hill.

Kat tried to smile, but her face felt frozen in a mask. What had she done wrong? She'd played to the crowd. Wasn't that what the team wanted?

Manager Addebary motioned them to the dugout. "Nice job, ladies. You've already got the locals eating out of your hands." Lola shoved a sharp elbow in Kat's side. She jumped away, rubbing the tender spot. "Go clean up at the hotel. We have a meeting in the lobby in an hour to match you with your host families. Then another practice. We leave for our first game tomorrow."

"Tomorrow?" Jackie groaned. "We won't have time to settle."

"That's not what you're paid for." Manager Addebary softened his words with a smirk. "You're here to play ball, and we'll play a lot of it this summer. Brace yourselves."

An hour later Kat walked into the lobby, insides quaking, and realized she was the last arrival again. She hoped her smile held steady, though she feared everyone could see through her. So much for the competent gal who belonged. Instead she felt the lack of each of her seventeen years. The others were older, more experienced. They'd know how to handle any situation thrown at them. She'd always lived at home in the same room with the same bed.

Older couples sat in the chairs set up in a semicircle. Kat edged next to Lola. "Have they told us anything yet?"

"If you can't get here on time, why should I tell you? I'm not your babysitter."

Kat stepped back, eyes wide. "I'm sorry." Did the woman handle stress by barking at anyone unfortunate enough to be near? Kat edged away and leaned against the wall behind a potted plant.

She sucked in one breath then another. *Father, please send me a friend. I don't know who to trust and if anybody cares.* She swallowed against the lump of tears that threatened. Time to "stiffen that upper lip" as Cassandra, Josie's foster daughter from London, liked to say.

Where had the confidence gone that flooded her on the field? There had to be more to her than a ball flying into her glove.

Addebary cleared his throat and stepped to the middle, his ample stomach hanging over the front of his belted slacks. "Thanks for coming. I'm delighted to introduce you fine folks to the women who make up the Cherry Hill Blossoms.

Although they will stay with you, I think you'll find they'll be busy and on the road much of the time. The season is short, intense, and packed with games. Joanie Devons here is our team chaperone. The girls already know her, and she'll work with each of you to make sure the girls follow the strict league rules. If you have any questions or need any interference run, Joanie's your gal."

With a prim smile Joanie stepped to the front. As the chaperone matched the team with families, Kat struggled to pay attention. Looked like Joanie had pulled her hair back so tight that her ears stood at attention. Did she get headaches from the tension? Kat shook her curls against her neck, glad for the freedom.

"Katherine Miller." Oh, time to focus. "Katherine is our youngest player, but I think you'll find her an easy addition to your home."

Kat pasted a smile on as she wondered whether Joanie had meant that as a compliment.

"Katherine, you'll be living with Mr. and Mrs. Wayne Harrison and their children."

The smile wavered as Kat counted heads. Several small ones peeked from behind the parents. Maybe road games wouldn't be so bad after all.

She looked away and stopped when she saw that insufferable Jack Raymond. The reporter seemed inclined to stalk her every move, and the wicked guffaw he unsuccessfully stifled made her face twist as if she'd just eaten one of Grandma's tart apples before it ripened. She tried to smooth the river of wrinkles from her forehead but couldn't. She forced her attention back to her hosts.

"Pleased to meet you." Kat looked into Mrs. Harrison's tired eyes, and the urge to ease the woman's burdens overwhelmed her. "I so appreciate you offering me space in your home for the summer."

"It's not much, but you're welcome to it." The thin woman

shrugged. "We'll give you as much peace as we can while you're in town."

They were just children. Surely she could handle living with them. "It will be fine. I'm sure of it."

The child with long, blond braids stuck out her tongue at Kat.

Maybe this wouldn't work after all. But Kat didn't have a chance to say anything. With a clap Addebary dismissed them.

"Thank you again for your hospitality, folks. Girls, don't forget practice begins in thirty minutes. Then you'll move to your new homes, and tomorrow we leave for our first games."

Mr. Harrison grabbed Kat's arm. "Would you like me to take anything to the house for you?"

"That's kind." Kat thought about what was in her room. "There's not much, so I'll bring it with me." Mrs. Harrison frowned, her gaze on his hand. Kat stepped away from his touch and hoped her smile softened the action. "Thank you. I'll come as soon as I can after practice."

"That'll be fine." Mrs. Harrison's expression softened. "We have dinner at five thirty sharp." She bit her lower lip. "If you can join us then."

"I'll get there as soon as I can. It depends on what manager Addebary has planned at practice." An unsettled feeling made Kat want to clutch her stomach.

Lola brushed past her, and Kat startled. "Keep standing there, and you'll be late."

The Harrisons stared after the gal. Mrs. Harrison shook her head. "Sorry to keep you. I've written our address down for you. Anybody can direct you."

"Thank you. I hate to run, but I can't be late for practice." Kat nodded at each of them. A tightness stilted her breathing. *Father, I don't have my mother's skill at welcoming people. Yet. Please help me be Your light in their family.* Her thoughts traveled to Lola. *And with Lola and the rest of the team. I feel so out of my element and alone.* A calm descended on her, and her breathing eased. She pushed the elevator button and savored the relaxed feeling.

God would not have asked her to do this if He wouldn't provide what she needed. He'd never promised this would be an easy journey. A good thing, since so far she felt more like a player suddenly surrounded by the opposing team during playoffs than someone confident in her skills.

As long as God went with her, she could do this. Somehow she could be His ambassador.

"Miss?" The girlish voice caused Kat to turn around.

"Yes?"

"Could I get your autograph?" A girl stood a few feet behind Kat, her stance tight, brown hair tugged into a tight ponytail. Dust coated her pants as if she'd slid into home a time or two that morning.

"Mine?" The girl must be looking for someone else.

"You're Katherine Miller, right?"

Kat nodded.

"Then you're who I want." The kid handed over the morning's paper and pointed at the photo.

Kat took the paper then looked up to see Jack watching her from the corner, a cocky grin on his face. She grabbed the pen the girl offered then scrawled a signature across the bottom of her picture. The girl walked off, whistling as she clutched the paper to her chest. An unsettled feeling squished Kat at the sight. The child was entirely too happy to have her signature. The elevator doors swooshed open. A hand held them open.

"See." Jack's word whispered against her hair, and a shiver shimmied down her spine.

Kat closed her eyes, trying not to enjoy his woodsy scent. "See what?"

"I can make you a star."

six

This was it. The first game of her professional career would begin in fifteen minutes. Kat pulled on the cream uniform for the Cherry Hill Blossoms. Her fingers tingled, and spots dotted her vision, part of her usual experience before a game started. She took deep breaths to push through the nerves.

"Who thought cream made a good color for a softball uniform?" Disgust laced Rosie's voice.

Lola guffawed. "They'll be tan before the fourth inning."

"Not if we dance from base to base." Jackie bounced on her toes, arms held in front of her in some ballet position.

Laughter swelled in the clubhouse. And with it Kat felt like she could take a deep breath for the first time since arriving in Racine. This wasn't the first game she'd played, but it felt like it. Someday she'd lose the voice in her head repeating all the times men had told her she didn't belong on the diamond. Then she'd lose the need to prove to everyone she'd earned a spot on the team. Maybe she'd believe she had the talent to contribute.

"Ladies, let's focus on the game rather than the uniforms." Joanie Devons, the always-perfect chaperone, clipped each word off precisely. The tittering died off in the face of her stiff words.

"Everyone decent in there?" Addebary's voice boomed into the room.

A girl squealed in one of the corners and yanked her uniform the rest of the way up. "Someone help me."

Kat moved over to help her button into the uniform. "We're set."

"Man coming in." Addebary eased into the room, a hand

over his eyes. He peeked through his fingers. "All right. Gather round." He waited while the team complied. "Ladies, tonight we have our opening game against the Racine Belles. You've practiced hard and are as ready as I can make you. Now it's time to go out there and become a team. You have to work together and focus on what we need to do to win.

"I'm proud of you. Now let's pray and go play ball."

Everybody took off their caps and bowed their heads. "Lord, we ask You to go with us. Help us do our best. Amen."

"And help us beat the Belles."

Kat smiled at Lola's addendum. That girl had vinegar flowing through her veins.

Kat's fingers trembled as she put her baseball cap back on. She needed to get a grip on herself. Lose this sense of unease and uncertainty.

"Are you gonna stare at your belly button all day or come play?"

Some days Kat wished she could smack Lola and her harsh attitude. Instead she smiled. "Let's play ball."

The women whooped and ran from the clubhouse. Kat stopped as soon as she reached the diamond. "Where are the fans?"

At most a couple hundred people sat in the stands, scattered around the bleachers.

"Guess we'll have to wow them with our playing prowess." Jackie smacked her gum, gloved hand propped on her hip.

"You're supposed to spit that out." Joanie frowned at Jackie.

"Miss Charm School isn't here, and I like playing with gum."

"Looks too much like chew. Hand it over." Joanie stuck out her hand, and Jackie spit the gum into it.

The girls marched onto the diamond and formed the victory formation with the Belles. They placed themselves in a V shape, proceeding from the point of home plate, and stood at attention while a Racine resident sang the national anthem. As visitors the Blossoms were at bat first. Kat rode the bench as other players took their turns at bat. Lola was up first. After a strike she hit a ball along the third baseline. Up next, Rosie got a pitch low and inside and drove it into left field. After them, two players struck out.

"Come on!" Lola yelled from second base. "Someone give me a hit to work with."

Faye marched to the plate, bat held firmly over her shoulder. She planted her feet and swung hard at the first pitch.

"Strike one!" The umpire held up the count.

Faye squared her shoulders and stared at the pitcher. The ball sailed toward her, and her bat connected with a resounding *whack*. Faye took off as her ball sailed into the outfield. Lola tore off the base and ran around third to home. She crossed home plate, Rosie sliding in behind her with a grimace.

The bench erupted. Two runs, two outs for the Blossoms.

Faye stood on second, ready to run with the next hit. Kat took a breath, slapped on a cap, and grabbed a bat to take a couple of practice swings on deck. This might be her first professional game, but she could do this. She'd spent a lifetime preparing. One more player stood in front of Kat, then she'd get her chance to knock one out of the park.

"Strike one!"

Kat focused on controlling her breathing as she took practice swings. In. Out. In. Out.

"Strike two!"

Kat looked up, noticed a line of sweat on Claudia's cheek. "Come on, Claudia. You can hit it." Kat's pulse quieted. She took a few more practice swings.

"Strike three!"

Claudia grimaced then marched from home plate.

"Better luck next time, Claud." A couple of players slapped her on the back, as she walked by them and they headed out to the field.

"Get on the field, girls."

Kat dropped the bat against the fence, collected her glove,

and then moved to her shortstop position. A calm settled on her. She could guard this slice of the diamond in her sleep.

The first Belle stepped to the plate and took her stance, bat held over her shoulder. Kat tried to watch her but found her gaze wandering around the stands. If the fans didn't pick up, the league couldn't last long no matter how deep Mr. Wrigley's pockets were.

Focus, Katherine Miller. Keep your eye on the ball.

Kat took a deep breath and sank deeper into her stance. She shifted her weight from side to side as she waited. The batter swung at a ball that sailed into the strike zone.

The umpire pumped his fist. "Strike one!"

The player whiffed another ball. "Strike two!"

"Come on, batter." A fan stood and leaned over the barrier. "Can't you see the ball?"

Fans around him shushed him, but the player grimaced. She squared her jaw, and fire lit her eyes. Kat watched her closely. Maybe she was mad enough now to hit the ball.

The batter swung. The bat connected. The ball sailed straight toward Kat. Kat leapt to the ball, expecting it to land in her glove. They always did. It flew past her mitt, and Kat turned to watch the left fielder and center fielder race for it. Her stomach clenched. She should have had that ball. Instead the batter made it to first base, and the fans cheered.

The man grinned. "See. I told ya you could do it." He dropped onto the bleacher with a grin.

Faye walked toward her, a ball playing through her fingers. "Come on, Kat. Get your head in the game."

Kat nodded. She had to get this right.

❧

By the fifth inning Jack felt as restless as the fans. The teams played well, but it really didn't seem much different from watching a church league, other than the fact the gals played in those ridiculous short skirts. He stood and made his way to the concession stand. A box of Cracker Jack and bottle of Coca-Cola later, he returned to his seat, not bothering to stifle a yawn.

What he wouldn't give to get a redo on the article he'd biffed, the one that got him fired from the Chicago paper and had him now covering titillating games like the one before him. He'd learned his lesson the hard way. Always double-check sources. Especially when the story involved a politician and a scandal.

He was a better reporter than this. His old editor knew it, too. Maybe he'd decided it was finally time to stop punishing him and let Jack return to the big leagues of Chicago.

Kat's playing disappointed him. The zest and magic she'd exhibited in team tryouts and practice had evaporated like the dew. All that remained were wispy hints that somewhere inside her the ballplayer lurked.

She'd have to improve under pressure before he could make her a star. And only then would he have the articles that would get his former editor's attention. That man wouldn't care about the girls' league without something more. No, he'd require a human-interest story that gripped readers and tugged them to games. Then he'd acknowledge that Jack's words had regained their power.

Jack shifted on the bench. The bench had left a permanent impression on his backside. Too bad they didn't have padding.

The game ended, with the Belles winning 4 to 3. The Blossoms looked deflated, but Addebary smiled as if content with the outcome.

"Come on, gals. Back to the hotel. We'll get you settled and do this all over again tomorrow."

Jack groaned. He didn't need the reminder that this was an away series. How would he kill time in Racine, Wisconsin? An idea hit him.

If he stuck close to the team, he could see if they lived by the strict rules.

No smoking or hard alcohol in public.

All social engagements approved ahead of time by the team chaperone.

No fraternization between players of different teams.

Just thinking through the never-ending list made him feel constrained. Jack doubted the players would last long with the laundry list.

It might be too early in the season, but at some point, the gals would resist the strict policies and be ready to find some fun. And when they did, he could be there ready to help publicize those slips.

His conscience pricked. He shouldn't go around looking for the worst in people. And his last attempt at investigative reporting had gotten him booted from Chicago. But the reality remained that people bought papers to see how others failed. He'd never succeed in shaking the dust of Cherry Hill from his shoes unless he gave readers the stories they wanted, no, expected.

Katherine Miller walked past, limping with dirt marring her skirt. She looked like she'd been bloodied by a neighborhood bully.

She'd fight back, find her footing.

❧

Kat groaned as Joanie doctored her leg.

"You've managed to give yourself a fine strawberry, Kat Miller." The woman tsked as she painted the wound with iodine, her touch surprisingly tender. "I don't know why you girls do this to yourselves."

Pain surged down her leg, and Kat bit back a scream.

"You'll have to re-hem your skirt. Looks like you didn't do too tight of a job."

"I've never liked sewing." Kat gritted her teeth and groaned.

"Maybe your host can help, but I'll see what I can do before tomorrow's game." Joanie patted her arm. "I think I'm done. Next."

Kat swung her legs over the side of the table and pushed off gingerly, favoring her bandaged leg.

"Coming to the hotel?" Lola waited inside the doorway, gear bag slung over her shoulder.

"Go ahead. I need to clean up a bit more."

"We may leave for dinner before you get back."

Kat nodded. "That's fine."

Right now all she wanted was a hot bath and bed. Maybe she'd wait to clean up until she got to the hotel. Several of the girls left as Kat eased around the clubhouse, collecting her gear.

She grabbed the last item and waved good-bye to the stragglers. "See you back at the hotel."

Joanie looked up from her latest victim and nodded. "Remember the rules."

"Yes, ma'am." This could be a long summer if she heard about the rules every time she turned around. She'd never needed so many rules before. Her parents expected her to obey them and honor her heavenly Father. That had always been sufficient. Now it looked like the regulations and monitoring would never end.

Jack Raymond lounged against the outside wall of the field house.

She tried to walk past him with a small wave. Right now she didn't want to weigh each word against how it would be construed in the newspaper. She also didn't want to pretend she was a model or movie star sashaying from the building. The thought of stiffening her back and holding her head erect with perfect posture like they'd preached in charm school hurt. She was too tired to do any of that. Instead slouching the few blocks to the hotel sounded wonderful.

Jack pushed away from the wall and stepped toward her. "Let me take you to dinner."

Kat stopped in her tracks, gear bag weighing heavy against her shoulder. "What?"

"You know. . .dinner, you and me. We have to eat, right?" He grinned, a smile that quirked up on the side. Kat imagined it stopped many girls in their tracks, but she bristled to think that he assumed it would work on her.

"I am not your typical woman, Mr. Raymond." Kat barreled past him.

"Hey, wait a minute." Jack picked up the pace to match hers. "I've never claimed you were a woman. You aren't even eighteen."

"No, but you'll make me a star, right? All I have to do is fall all over you and act like I can't think of anything better than spending time with you." Heat flamed in her face, and Kat wanted to bite her tongue before it got away from her. But she couldn't. She turned, planted her hands on her hips, and watched him crash to a stop. "I've no interest in whatever you have to offer."

"You think I'm propositioning you." His neck turned a dangerous red, and he clenched his fists against his waist. Kat tried to ignore the power of his stance, and the hard lines that planed his face.

"Aren't you?"

He stomped away from her and back. "What rock did you climb out from under? It is possible for a man and a girl to have dinner without ulterior motives."

Did he mean it? Kat eyed him, unsure what to do. A wave of fatigue swamped her. She swayed, and he steadied her arm. A shock wave of electricity bolted up her arm. She tugged free. "I have to go." She raced down the block toward the hotel, fatigue washed away by the sense she had to get distance.

What had happened?

As her heart pulsed, she didn't want to answer the question. *God, help me.* She'd never felt such an intense emotion from one touch.

She couldn't allow her heart to follow the feeling. Jack Raymond was older—and couldn't possibly see her as anything other than a story. Why he even saw her that way, she couldn't understand. Faye was certainly prettier. Lola more confident. Anybody a better player.

Kat steeled her heart. She was here to play ball. She couldn't open her heart to a summer romance with a man she wouldn't see after the season ended. Not when she'd guarded it carefully so far.

Pushing through the hotel's door, she raced through the lobby and up the stairs to her room. She unlocked the door and collapsed on the bed.

"What got into you?" Lola gaped at her from her bed. "You're white as a new softball."

"Nothing."

A knowing expression crossed Lola's face. "Does that nothing go by the handle *Jack Raymond*?"

Kat shrugged.

"Watch yourself with him. You're too innocent to spend time with a man."

seven

"Raymond, this isn't good enough." Ed tossed the sheets of paper on his desk. "I've had you follow the Blossoms all over a tristate area so you could tell the good citizens of Cherry Hill why they should spend their hard-earned money and rare free time at Memorial Field, watching the girls play. This"—he gestured at the paper—"drivel doesn't hack it."

Jack stood in front of the editor's battered desk, pressure building at his temples. How long would the tirade go on this time?

"I could keep you here covering town hall and let Meredith over there follow the team. Bet she'd find the human-interest stories. Or better yet, I'll get stringers in each town. Save the paper a boatload of money we're throwing away on you and your outlandish expenses."

A muscle tightened in his jaw. "I've written good stories covering the games."

"Sure. Play-by-play is exactly what our readers want. Has them racing to the stands to buy the paper. They can get that on the radio." Ed shook his head. "We've got to offer them something they can't get anywhere else. There's too much competition for anything less." He crossed his arms and leaned over his desk. "Look, kid, I know this isn't your final destination. But if this is all you've got to pour on the page, it will be. Now get out there, and find me something I can print."

Jack strode from the room, easing the door shut behind him rather than slamming it like he wanted. He walked across the small newsroom to the reporters' bays, strides hamstrung like his writing. Four desks set in a square formation, phones and piles of papers marring each surface. He grabbed the gray fedora from his desk, slammed it on his head, and headed out the door.

"Where you headed?" Doreen Mitchell, the receptionist and gal of all trades, queried before he could sneak away.

"Out."

"Told you couldn't find a story again?" The light of sympathy in her gaze was the last thing he wanted.

"Research."

"Uh-huh."

"I'll be back in an hour."

"You'll need this." She tossed him a pad and pen. "Good luck."

"Thanks."

What he really needed was every bit of luck he could get.

Main Street didn't look alive, not in between festivals. The cherry blossom festival had ended in April, and with it the tourists had abandoned the town until the next festival in July. Now the regulars focused on work—long shifts at the factories on the outskirts of town that the town fathers had turned into munitions shops. All civilian activities had morphed into something that aided the war effort.

Then there was him. Stuck hunting for a ridiculous series of human-interest stories about girls playing softball. Good grief. Made him want to hunt for another line of work. Until he considered his options, that was. Spending all day standing and sweltering in a superheated factory wouldn't work with his knee any better than combat.

His was in a lose-lose situation. No getting around it.

So write stories about the girls he would. Even that was better than covering another town hall meeting.

He continued down Main Street, looking for anything that would prompt a story idea. The suits in the haberdashery's window looked outdated. Nobody had parked cars in front of the First Bank of Cherry Hill. He walked past more establishments. Jorgenson's Furniture. Behr's Soda Fountain. The five-and-dime. He stopped to scan the five-and-dime's window, but nothing caught his eye.

Jack Raymond did not struggle to find topics. But the Jack Raymond of old also didn't have women unaffected by his presence.

He stopped cold. Where had that thought slunk from?

He needed to clear his mind of one Katherine Miller. She was practically in diapers. Hadn't even graduated from high school.

But he couldn't clear his mind of her when her profile languished in his notebook.

Ed was right. Each of his reports focusing on the game alone fell flat. They were accurate reflections of the game but missed the heart. With a girls' team, that should be easy to capture. The way they gave their all to every play. The way they raced around the bases, tongues caught between their teeth as they determined to make it to home regardless of what stood in their way. The way they played hard after the game.

There was a thought.

He shoved his hands in his pockets and started walking, head down in concentration. His mind played with the idea. Some of them played mighty hard. In violation of the rules. . .

The sound of heels clicking along the sidewalk registered right before he collided with someone. He looked up and stopped. Looked like he'd conjured up a Blossom, just not the one that filled his thoughts with her athletic form and smile.

A woman sat on the ground shaking her head. For a moment he hoped he'd see auburn curls under the sporty hat. Instead a soft brown bob peeked out.

Faye Donahue shook her head then stared at him with doe eyes. "Mr. Raymond, would you mind assisting me to my feet?" A flirty smile had him grinning in reply.

"Certainly." He pulled her to her feet, surprised by how

light she felt. "Are you okay?"

"I'm a softball player. It would take more than your tap to hurt me." Faye brushed off her skirt. "Well, good day."

"Wait." Jack tapped his pad of paper. "Would you like a cherry Coke at Behr's? I wondered if I might profile you, the team's dazzling pitcher, in my next article."

"Any plans to highlight my tomboy antics?"

Jack winced as she threw his words from the prior article back at him. "Or should I tell everyone you performed in a circus?"

"I thought you might focus on the beauty kit. You know, 'avoid noisy, rough, and raucous talk and actions. . . .'"

"I like your sense of humor. Looks like I'll need to be more over the top." He opened the door to Behr's and let her proceed. "How about a banana split?"

❧

Kat didn't think she could take another moment. When awake she practiced or played in games in Cherry Hill or on the road, always surrounded by her teammates. When at home, the Harrison children kept things hopping at the house. The only place she could relax was church. Even there, she sensed people watching her—mainly with curiosity, but some looks bordered on hostility. She went to worship and remember the great sacrifice made for her.

Right now she needed peace and quiet away from others. Even an hour would do.

She hurried down Main, a tote slung over her shoulder, wearing a simple skirt and blouse. Just once she wished she could wear shorts or pants in public, but this summer she had to follow the rules. At all times. The consequences of not obeying—being sent home to Dayton—were unacceptable. She might long for some peace and quiet, but she loved every moment on the diamond. That magical experience of playing a game she loved in front of fans who wanted to see the AAGPSL teams play continued to make her feel alive.

Ahead of her a group exited the drugstore, and she slowed to let them past. A laugh caught her attention. Faye leaned on Jack Raymond's arm, giggling as he gestured while they left the store. Kat's heart stalled, and she quickly turned to look into the store's plate glass window. Her heart tightened, and she struggled to pull in a breath. The crazy reaction only reinforced her need for time alone.

The couple strolled past, but Kat kept her focus on the window. After they'd walked down the sidewalk, she turned to watch and caught Jack looking over his shoulder at her. He tipped his hat, and heat crawled up her neck.

Argh. She turned and stomped toward the park.

"Stupid girl," she muttered as she marched. This had to stop. Time to get a grip on her zigzagging, roiling emotions.

Kat reached the park and slowed her pace. A picnic table sitting in a pool of dappled sunlight pulled at her. A breeze blew through a stand of elms a few feet away, taking the edge off the heat. Children ran around a merry-go-round, their laughter filling the air. She sank onto the bench, and a bird tittered from a branch overhead.

Stillness settled over Kat as she soaked in the atmosphere. She closed her eyes, breathed deep, and quieted her heart.

Father, I'm sorry I've let so many days pass without making time with You a priority. Forgive me? Make me hungry for You. Prompt me until I can't let a day end without seeking You.

She kept her eyes closed and waited. The silence and peace enveloped her. Something rubbery plunked against her thigh. She opened her eyes, looked down, and found a dodge ball next to her.

Chucking it to a young boy who stood a few feet away watching her, she then opened her bag and pulled out her Bible. Kat opened it to her favorite passage, Psalm 40.

As she read yet again the words she'd memorized, they resonated in her spirit.

"I waited patiently for the LORD; and he inclined unto me, and

heard my cry." Her eyes scanned down to verse 4: "*Blessed is that man that maketh the* L*ORD his trust, and respecteth not the proud, nor such as turn aside to lies.*"

She tilted her face toward the sun. *Lord, help me to always trust in You, first and foremost in my life. I don't want to live like the proud and find myself pulled away by any god other than You.*

Any god other than Him. What did that mean? It wasn't like she would walk away and abandon God or stop going to church. What was a god? Something people exalted in their lives. That made the possibilities almost endless.

Softball?

Kat cringed. Softball was a game. Not something she worshipped. Then she considered every day that she'd made time to practice. Rushed to pack a bag and catch the train that would take her to the next city and the next game. Maybe the thought wasn't as far-fetched as she'd like. *Father, forgive me.*

Verse by verse she meditated on the psalm, celebrating the way the words came to life with meaning. When she reached verse 10, she stopped and read it again. "*I have not hid thy righteousness within my heart; I have declared thy faithfulness and thy salvation: I have not concealed thy lovingkindness and thy truth from the great congregation.*"

The words stabbed her.

How many times had she failed to speak up when given the opportunity to share the goodness and faithfulness of God? To explain the great kindness He showed in His efforts to draw people to Him?

Maybe the reason she played on the Blossoms was to reveal His righteousness and faithfulness. She studied the thought, let it penetrate her heart.

Had she ever bothered to help her hosts beyond the basic role of a guest? Mrs. Harrison lived on the edge of poverty, overwhelmed with her household of children, yet had opened her home anyway. Kat vowed to find ways to help her. She needed to live beyond her comfort and take advantage of each opportunity God gave her.

God had her in Cherry Hill for a reason. One that extended far beyond playing a game. She knew that to the core of her being.

Now she needed to live like she believed it.

"Ah, so this is where you hide."

Kat started, hand placed over her heart, at the sudden deep voice. She spun on the bench and found herself staring into Jack Raymond's dark eyes. "What are you doing here?" She refrained from asking where Faye had gone.

"Thinking." Jack shrugged, his hands tucked firmly in his pockets. "May I join you?" He sank beside her before she could protest, even if she'd wanted to. "You are a puzzle, Miss Miller."

"I am?"

"Yes. You seem so above the competition that pushes so many of the girls on the team. But you're still filled with passion."

"I love softball."

He nodded. "That's clear from the moment you step on the diamond. Why? It's a game."

Kat shrugged. "I'm here for a reason."

The look he shot her told her exactly what he thought of that statement. A bit too obvious. "Everybody is."

"No. I mean I believe God has me here. I'm not sure exactly why, but I intend to play as hard as I can for as long as I can."

"With a war raging across the world, I doubt He cares all that much about your softball games. He's a bit distracted by weightier matters."

"Do you really believe that?" Kat studied him, longing to know the answer.

"Yes. I can't see how things could be different."

"Do you go to church?"

"Sure."

Kat considered him a moment. Was this one of those times God wanted her to say something? Or should she let it drop? His face seemed open, as if he wanted to hear what she'd say. *Please don't let it be one of his reporter tricks designed to get a rise out of me to give him plenty of information for one of his articles.* "If God cared enough about each of us to send His only Son to die for us, then I think He cares about what happens in our day-to-day lives. I was just reading a psalm that talks about God listening to us when we cry to Him. It didn't say anything about the request needing to be a certain level before He notices."

The words settled in the air around them for a minute. The silence felt comfortable, nonthreatening. As if she were talking to her brother Mark about a weighty topic.

"You know this won't last." Jack broke the silence, his gaze gauging her reaction.

"Why do you say that?"

"If more fans don't fill the seats, the league won't make it past this season. Simple economics at play. If there aren't enough tickets sold, there isn't enough revenue to cover the costs, let alone make a profit. The town fathers can't support it for long without some financial payback."

"It'll come." It had to.

eight

"Do you think he meant it?" Rosie lolled against the bench in the Blossoms' clubhouse.

"Of course he did." Lola chomped on her gum, the grimace pasted on her face. "It doesn't take a genius to figure out there aren't enough people in the stands most days."

"Ladies, please watch your tone." Joanie paused in doctoring a strawberry on Faye's leg and gave Lola and Rosie the evil eye. "You needn't worry about the business structure of the league."

Kat listened to the exchange between the players and chaperone but didn't agree with Joanie's conclusion. If there weren't enough spectators, there wouldn't be a team. Much as the experience stretched her, she didn't want to return to Dayton and spend the rest of the summer playing an occasional game with the boys and helping Mother around the house.

With her older sister, Josie, and her kids back home while Art served in the army, home felt cramped. Add in Mark and his crazy hours at the National Cash Register Company working on his top-secret project, and she might have a bit more privacy living with strangers. Well, not actually.

No, this summer formed an opportunity to stretch her wings and fulfill a dream.

There must be something they could do to keep the league viable. "Are we active enough in the community?"

Her teammates turned and stared at Kat.

"I think my photo's in more than enough ads." Faye posed, arm pulled back as if to throw, big grin plastered on her face.

"Well, I think you're a beast, not sharing more of the camera time with the rest of us." Claudia stuck her tongue out at Faye. "Do you have to hog so much?"

"Some days you girls are too much for a body to handle. Worried about who has the most pictures in the paper. Good night." Joanie shook her head. "Y'all need to pack and be at the train station in two hours. I'm taking a break. See you at the station." She grabbed her hat and purse and huffed out of the room, letting the door slam behind her.

Lola plopped down next to Kat. "You're a cute kid, but what on earth do you think we could do?"

"Make more community appearances, maybe?"

Faye shook her head. "We're already running all the time. If we're not practicing, we're packing for a game. If we're not in town trying to humor our host families, we're on a train headed to another small city that looks an awful lot like Cherry Hill. I barely find time to sleep as it is."

Others nodded and murmured among themselves.

Maybe she should wait until she had a well-formed idea to share with them. Kat stood but sat down again as Addebary barreled into the clubhouse.

"Girls, if all goes well with our trains, we'll play the Rockford Peaches tonight. They're a good team, so I want to see your best. All of it. Every slide you've held back, make it tonight. We've got three games to beat one of the leading teams.

"And we've got company on this trip."

Excitement rippled through the room. Kat couldn't imagine who would join them and why the others would think company was what they needed.

"Jack Raymond will join us on this trip. He'll be with you all the time, except when you're sleeping, of course." Addebary stared at each of them. "No fraternizing with the reporter in any kind of intimate way. He is here to learn more about each of you for a series of special stories he's writing. If it'll get more fans here to watch you play, it's a good thing. Now get going, and don't forget your gear."

After a mad scramble, the room emptied, except for Kat. She

remained rooted to the bench, leaning against the cold, metal locker. Jack Raymond. Traveling with them. That annoying, self-absorbed reporter. She wouldn't have a moment's peace with him there determined to make her a star. She couldn't take it. Not now.

All the peace she'd clung to since her time with God in the park threatened to abandon her. *God, help me cling to You and Your peace.*

❧

Traveling on a train with that gaggle of girls. He must be desperate for a story. Jack had written a puff piece on Faye Donahue and left it along with his profile of Katherine Miller on Ed's desk. The man would have to be satisfied with them for now.

In his small apartment, really just a room behind a garage, Jack busily stuffed clothes and underwear in a satchel. Three days. Then he'd return to his abode if Ed didn't send him on to the next road series with the Blossoms. Some American dream. A twelve-by-twelve space with a bed, dresser, and hot plate. At least his dreams exceeded the scope of this town. Someday he'd shake the dust from his shoes and return to a real city. He could already smell the Windy City's unique, deep-dish pizza and numerous hot dog stands.

Yep, that was the ticket.

A knock sounded on his door, and Jack looked up from his packing. Who could it be? No one ever visited him, and as he looked at the piles of laundry on the floor and dirty dishes in the sink, he hoped it wasn't anyone important. Whoever it was knocked again. "Just a minute."

Jack grabbed an armful of dirty clothes and shoved them in the bottom drawer of the dresser where they'd have to wait until his return. He strode to the door and opened it. "Polly."

"Hi, Jack. Can I come in?" Her gaze searched his face, her curls playing across her forehead and tempting him to brush them away.

"Sure." He stumbled back to let her pass. "I've got to get to the train station."

"Ed warned me." Polly glanced around, as if looking for a place to sit then leaned against the wall instead. "Jack, what's happened?"

"What do you mean?"

"I know we didn't spend all our time together, but since the Blossoms came to town, I never see you." She crossed her arms, a pretty pout playing on her mouth. "Has one of them captured your attention? Become your girl?"

Jack ran his fingers through his hair and avoided eye contact. It wasn't like he had a serious relationship with any of them. "Ed's had me traveling with the team."

"So. . ."

"Polly. . ."

"Are you leaving me, Jack?"

"I don't plan to live in Cherry Hill a minute longer than needed."

She turned her back to him. "That answers my question."

The pain in her voice made him wonder if he should backpedal. "I've never said I wanted this to be my only job."

"But I've been part of your future, haven't I?"

"Polly, I sent a letter to the United Press this week. One of these days I'll get an assignment with a news service or paper in a bigger city. I don't know when or where, but that's my goal. Things are too uncertain to make any promises to you." He shoved his hands in his pockets. Should he walk over to her? But he didn't want to give her the wrong impression, and it sounded like she'd already had them walking down the aisle—something that had never been his intention. "I'm sorry, Polly."

She held up her hand to stop him then swiped under her eyes. "I'll leave now." She thrust her chin up and stepped to the door. "You might consider a maid. Good-bye, Jack."

Jack watched her walk away, surprised that he had no

desire to follow her. He glanced at his watch and startled. He needed to be at that train station now.

He shoved another pair of socks into the bag then zipped it shut. Jack grabbed the bag and headed out. After locking the door he walked to the train station. This time the Blossoms were off to Rockford, then they'd be home for a week.

Team members had entered the station a few minutes before he arrived. Kat leaned against the wall looking tired, dark circles discoloring the area under her eyes. She must have lost her powder puff.

Kat fit the bill for a good kid. The cuteness element played heavily in her favor. From the freckles dotting her nose, to the dimple in her chin and the sparkle in her green eyes, she magnetized guys' attention without thought. She probably walked around town oblivious to her power. A good thing, too, or she'd lose some charm by wielding it as a tool. Guys would do a double take at her photo, and young women wouldn't feel threatened by her since she played such an unfeminine game, skirts aside. Jack only wished she weren't so boring. Her favorite activities revolved around church. Choir. Youth activities. Mission board. Yawn. Where was the newsworthy story in all that goodness? She'd never do anything that would make her look like anything other than the goody-two-shoes life she led.

Still, she was human. Eventually he'd find her Achilles' heel.

Everyone had one. Some required more digging than others, but it always existed.

His grandmother would be horrified if she knew the direction of his thoughts. The woman believed everyone could be a saint and anyone who confessed faith in Christ would live a life above reproach. He used to believe she was right.

Now he wasn't so sure. He'd seen too much of the underbelly of life. People who wanted to take from others all the time, who thought only of themselves and did for others only when it suited them.

Everyone had an angle.

Kat wouldn't be any different. She yawned so wide he waited for her jaw to pop. When she rubbed her jaw, he stifled a grin. Her frown let him know she'd caught him.

How could he be so cynical about someone as cute and wholesome as Kat?

Time to get on the train and away from his thoughts. Maybe today he'd join one of the card games. Chat it up with the team. He'd find the angles. Write the articles Ed wanted. Get back to Cherry Hill as soon as the series ended. Watch Kat.

Lola plopped into a seat and patted the one next to her. Kat sank onto it like an obedient kid. He hadn't figured Lola out yet. A great ballplayer but with a definite chip on her shoulder, one that she directed toward Kat. Why the kid followed Lola around, he didn't understand. If Kat slipped, it would be thanks to that woman.

The girl pulled out her bag and grabbed a book. Black leather cover worn around the edges. Had to be her Bible. Jack tucked his bag overhead and walked toward them. She'd buried her nose in the book and read it like it absorbed her attention. Poor thing, though he remembered days he'd read it with the same intensity.

Everyone had an angle.

A ballplayer's angle had cost him his first job in Chicago. He wouldn't let that happen again. The longer Kat stayed on the team, the more likely she'd step away from her faith and the real girl would come out.

Nothing against her. That's just the way it worked.

Get out, stretch your wings, and decide if faith was yours or your parents'.

Man, he'd turned into a cynic. Part of him hoped he was wrong. He liked what he'd seen.

A few days on the road provided the perfect opportunity

to see if Katherine's faith held up when she thought no one watched.

Part of him hoped she'd withstand the temptations. The other part knew it'd create a great story if she fell.

And he hated himself for that.

"Get a grip, Raymond." The train lurched, the motion throwing him into a seat. Girls tittered as he righted himself. Time to get this show on the road and his thoughts under control. It wasn't like he had a right to worry over Kat.

He needed to focus on what he did best. . .writing.

❧

The train jostled from side to side, and Kat swayed with it, a second-nature action after several weeks on and off the passenger cars. She watched as four of the girls played poker for pennies. Another foursome had set up a game of bridge. Jack Raymond had edged toward them and watched the action from a seat toward the back of the car. Every once in a while he wrote something on his ever-present notepad. He caught her watching and winked.

Heat crept up her neck, and she knew he had to see. A curse with her fair skin. Enough of this silliness. If he wanted to play that way, she'd join him. His eyes flashed with surprise as she sat next to him. "Ready for another round of games?"

"Have plans to slide into home again?" He grimaced as if reliving her last slide in his mind.

Kat rubbed her thigh, where the bruise had eased to yellows and greens. "I never plan to do it, you know. But I have to make it home."

He shook his head. "I still think you're crazy to do that in that dress."

"What choice do I have? I want to play, and that's the only way to do it." She turned toward him and grinned. "Though I've considered adding a pillow under the skirt. What do you think about that?"

Jack belly laughed. "You are a piece of work, Miss Miller."

How was she supposed to take that? She hadn't said anything wrong, had she?

He pulled a pack of cards from his jacket. "How about a card game?"

"I don't gamble."

"That's fine. How about pitch or euchre?"

"I think softball is more my style." His brow wrinkled at her words. "I mean, I don't know how to play either."

"That's a problem I can fix." He watched her a moment. "There's a lot you don't know, kid."

Her pulse hiccupped, even as she tensed at his word choice. She didn't want him to see her as a kid. The realization stopped her, and she scooted back on her seat. Maybe spending time with him, even in a group like this, was a terrible idea. He must have seen something in her face because he leaned closer, his breath warm on her neck.

"Someone's going to update your education. Be careful who you trust." He opened the box of cards and flipped them around. He shuffled them without breaking eye contact.

Kat jumped up, the book falling from her lap. "I—I need to do something." A dumb thing to say, but she couldn't think of anything coherent.

He leaned over and grabbed her Bible. She cringed as he carelessly tossed it onto the seat. "This'll be waiting for you when you come back."

She couldn't think but knew she had to break the sudden connection with Jack. Spinning on her heel, she fled down the aisle, colliding with Joanie. The woman ricocheted off a seat back, but Kat didn't stop. If she did, she might not get away.

They arrived in town in time for a quick practice before it got too dark. After practice everyone scrambled to change before heading out to find dinner.

"Come on, you slowpoke. We're going to the place across the street to eat." Rosie grinned at her. "If you don't hurry, you'll miss out."

The train had arrived too late for the game. A night of freedom was so rare that the clubhouse buzzed with excitement.

"You'll join us, won't you, Kat?" Faye smiled at her, seeming to want her to join them. "We'll be back in time for curfew."

"Sure. I'll be there in a bit." Kat started tugging off her dirty practice uniform as the first group of Blossoms headed out the door. She savored the warm shower before slipping into clean clothes. Part of her longed for the quiet of her hotel room. She'd enjoy a few minutes of solitude before her roommate returned, but it felt good to be included by the others. What would it hurt to pop over and join them for a bit? She walked across the street but stilled when she reached the establishment. Harry's Pub and Grill.

A stone settled in her stomach. This wasn't what she'd had in mind when she'd agreed to stop by the restaurant. She'd imagined a mom-and-pop kind of place.

Kat stood at the door of the "restaurant." What should she do?

If she didn't go in, the others would never let her live it down. If she did, she'd be breaking every rule and could be sent home. And that didn't begin to address the way it would reflect on her faith.

Sighing, she sank to the stoop outside the door. She couldn't go in.

Clouds rolled across the moon, and Kat shivered. How long would the others be in there? Music started, and she could hear the beat of dancing feet. Crazy laughter bounced out the open windows. Maybe she should walk to the hotel. It couldn't be that far.

Kat squinted into the darkness. A creeping chill stood the hair on her arms on end. So much for being brave. The longer she looked at the shadows, the more sinister they turned.

She lurched to her feet and then hurried inside. Cigarette smoke filled the crowded establishment. Kat coughed to clear her lungs.

"There you are." Rosie giggled as she danced by in the arms of a whiskered man. "You're missing all the fun."

"Maybe." Kat shrugged. "Are y'all ready to leave?"

Rosie danced away, as if she hadn't heard.

Most of the tables were occupied without an open chair. Kat squinted trying to find a seat then eyed the door. Maybe she should leave. The oppressive darkness kept her rooted in place. She glanced back around the room then stopped, spine stiffening. Jack Raymond sat at a table, Lola practically in his lap.

He winked at her, motioning to the vacant chair on the other side of him. If he thought she would subject herself to his company, he was sorely mistaken. She'd rather brave the unknown out there than watch him.

Kat spun on her heel and pushed through the door. Irrational pain sliced through her.

She needed an escape. Before this man wormed his way deeper into her life.

nine

The series with the Rockford Peaches behind them, the team moved to Joliet for another away series. For the first game Jack settled onto a bleacher, bag of popcorn and bottle of Coke tucked under an arm, a clump of hair spilling over his forehead into his eyes. Kat pulled her attention from him and shoved her right hand deeper into her glove. She had to focus on the game. The Blossoms led the game five to four in the bottom of the ninth, but the Jewels could turn the game around. One hit: That's all it took to tie and send the game into extra innings. She refused to imagine the Joliet team scoring more than one run.

As sweat dripped between her eyes, Kat prayed they'd avoid extra innings. The June heat and humidity had turned brutal.

She needed a tall glass of water to replace the buckets she sweated while the sun beat down on the field. She tugged off her hat, swiped her hand across her forehead, then replaced it and focused on the game. The league paid her to play, not complain.

Kat leaned forward in her position, eyes locked on the hitter. Ruth Maines, the Joliet Jewels' star, took the batter's stance and focused on Faye. Faye wound up then released the pitch. The ball sailed right at the bat. Ruth stepped into it and connected with a *crack*. The fans leaped to their feet with a roar that Kat silenced as she jumped into the air and snagged the ball. Adrenaline pulsed through her, and she tossed the ball to Lola at third base who continued throwing it around the horn until it was returned to Faye.

"Great job, Kat!" Rosie yelled from second base, a huge

grin on her face. "Two more like that, and we're home free."

The few loyal Blossoms fans who'd trekked from Cherry Hill whooped and hollered from their spots in the stands. Two more outs and the Blossoms would sew up the game. Kat wanted this win. Their lopsided losses ensured the Blossoms needed every win from here to the end of the season if they wanted any real chance in the playoffs.

Two Jewels had base hits that got them to first and second. Kat watched as their balls sailed into the outfield where she couldn't do a thing except grit her teeth and pray her teammates had sure hands.

With two strikes on the next batter, the runner on second broke for third. Kat had been caught off guard. If she'd crept up behind her and signaled to the catcher, they could have picked the runner off. The runner on first took second. Now the Blossoms were in hot water.

Kat shot a look at Lola who groaned on the ground next to third base. The player had raced into her, knocking Lola off her feet. Kat brushed her hands against her thighs then gave Lola a hand up. Lola swayed a moment then waved that she was okay.

That was one tough woman.

Kat shook her head and focused back on the hitter. Dolly? Had she already been transferred from Racine to Joliet? Kat knew some teams had traded players, but the Blossoms had avoided that so far. Dolly could hit a ball out of the park, so Kat wouldn't be able to do much if she connected with the ball. Faye must have remembered Dolly's skill because her first two pitches were off the plate.

If Dolly walked, the bases would be loaded. The next batter for the Jewels had a reputation for being an easy out with lots of pop flies. With two outs, walking Dolly kept her from hitting a home run and gave the Blossoms an opportunity for an easier out with the next hitter.

Two more balls, and Dolly moved to first.

Kat rolled her neck, tension pushing a headache from the back of her neck to her forehead. Faye wound up, a frown on her face but not the usual one that reflected her intense concentration. Instead it looked like something bothered her. Faye shot the ball across the plate, but the Jewel connected with the ball sending it straight at Kat. Kat moved to grab the ball with her glove, but in the muggy air she felt like she was pushing through molasses. The ball whizzed past her glove and sailed by her.

She scrambled to turn around, but her foot caught on a divot of some sort. Kat landed on her rear end. Rosie slipped in from her spot filling in at left field and flung the ball over Kat to Ruth at home. Despite Rosie's efforts, the gal from third base slid into home. Kat hung her head and groaned.

"I should have caught that." Kat glanced at the scoreboard: 5–5. Thanks to her botched effort. She fought the sensation that a sack of practice balls had dropped in her stomach. A torrent of sweat poured from her forehead. She swiped at it and tried to pull her thoughts back to the moment. Nothing she did would change what had happened. But she could impact what came next. She had to.

The next batter hit a home run, and the game was over.

The air rushed from Kat's lungs, and she struggled to stay on her feet. They'd been so close. She trudged in to join the rest of the team as they congratulated the Jewels. She mouthed the right words but had a hard time putting her heart into them. Just once, she'd like to win more than one game. It had been awhile since the Blossoms had managed that much.

Dolly grinned as she slapped hands with Kat. "Meet me for dinner?"

That sounded wonderful, but the rules said she couldn't. No fraternization between teams. What did it matter? Would the players really lose their desire to win if they became friends with opposing players? Kat sighed. It didn't matter what she thought. "You know I can't, Dolly."

The gal's face fell. "You're right. I hoped to spend a few minutes with a friendly face, that's all."

"I'd like it, too." Kat hugged Dolly. "I didn't know you were a Jewel."

"I didn't either until two days ago. One day I'm in Racine; the next I'm on a train to Joliet. I didn't even know such a place existed until this season." She tried to act nonchalant, but the slump in her shoulders told Kat the change was lonely.

A throat cleared behind Kat, and she turned to see Joanie standing there, arms crossed and a frown on her face. "Joining us, Miss Miller?"

The tone in her voice irritated Kat. She made a decision and turned back to Dolly. "Where are you going for dinner?"

Dolly's eyes widened, and a spark filled them. "The gals picked a favorite hangout across from your hotel. Maybe it's strategic for times like this."

"I'll see if I can slip away."

"Katherine Miller. The team is leaving. Now."

Kat squeezed Dolly one more time then stepped away. "I'll try to make it."

Dolly winked at her then hurried to join her teammates.

❧

The kid was scheming. It was as clear as the score on the scoreboard that Kat was up to something with that Jewel. He vaguely remembered seeing them together at spring training.

The chaperone really should temper her harsh edges, because Kat bristled each time she issued a demand. He couldn't imagine living under the rules, especially with the strict limitations. Kat's age seemed to keep her separated from her teammates, and Joanie didn't help matters any. He hadn't figured out her angle yet, but he would. Maybe it was as simple as being a frustrated ballplayer.

Whatever the cause, he followed Kat for a bit before

deciding he'd rather walk with her.

"Miss Miller."

She spun around at his words. "Please don't call me that. She's"—Kat jerked her chin toward the chaperone—"the only one who calls me that."

"Bad connotations."

"You could say that."

"Sorry about the loss, kid. You kept it close."

She snorted. "Until the last inning. How do we do that? We're so close to winning, and then we self-destruct. It's so frustrating."

"How about dinner? I'll distract you from your loss." He raised his hands before she could protest and put on his most charming smile, the one Polly used to liken to William Holden's. "We can call it an interview if that makes you feel better."

Kat stopped and studied him a moment before a gleam appeared in her eyes. "If you can talk Joanie into it, I'm in. And you have to take me to the restaurant next to our hotel."

"Why?"

"Let's just say I have my reasons."

Jack considered her words. An angle. Somewhere in them. Suddenly he knew. "So you can meet Dolly."

"Shh." Kat looked around, probably not realizing how guilty her actions looked.

"All right. You've got a deal. Clean up and meet me in the lobby. I'll talk to Joanie." His charm always worked on her. "We'll get you out for some fraternization."

Jack cooled his heels in the lobby while Kat changed. As he waited, he scanned the newspaper. The Joliet outfit wasn't much bigger than Cherry Hill's but seemed to have more true news stories. The war had heated up in Africa, and he longed to cover the story. He imagined hot sand pelting his face as he hunkered down behind a sand dune. There had to be a way to get to the real action, stop covering the foolishness of the AAGPSL, and cover something that mattered.

Maybe the letter he'd sent off to the United Press International would amount to something this time. A guy had to hope.

Kat swept down the stairs, gorgeous in a fitted blouse and billowing skirt. Delicate slippers encased her feet, and the curls on her head dripped at the edges. She had no idea she stole his breath. When was the last time he'd felt this way about Polly? Maybe it was a good thing—a very good thing—that she'd ended their tentative relationship. Kat's eyebrows shot up as she caught his gaze. He wiped his expression of surprise and offered her his arm.

"You look great." Her hand rested lightly on his arm, so he tucked his hand on top. He wouldn't let this bird fly away.

A soft smile touched her lips, easing the shadow that rested under her eyes. "Thank you."

He cleared his throat and ushered her to the door. "I hear the restaurant next door is good."

"Let's go." She grinned at him, an impish look. "I hope you brought plenty of cash. I'm as hungry as a horse. Losing does that to me."

Having her on his arm, he didn't care about a job overseas or the state of his cash. He only wanted to prolong the moment. They teased each other as they walked across the parking lot.

"The crowd seems enthusiastic." Kat's steps stuttered as if she had lost her footing. He glanced at her, surprised to see her cheeks devoid of color.

"Are the rumors true?" She licked her lips, tucking her bottom lip between her teeth. "Will they close the league if attendance doesn't improve?"

They reached the restaurant, and Jack opened the door. "Mr. Wrigley's got his eye set on making money. That's the ultimate goal of any venture like this."

"I wish playing a good game were sufficient." Kat bobbled

through the door then waited for Jack. "He's changing the league's name. Like substituting the word *baseball* for *softball* will suddenly draw hundreds of people."

"What could it hurt?" Something had to change. Today's game had more fans than most. He wondered if that was a feature of Joliet or meant a positive change for the league as a whole. For Kat's sake, he hoped it signaled a league-wide change.

Kat remained silent, and he glanced at her. In an instant he realized he might as well disappear. Her attention focused on a table in the back. "Dolly!" Kat squealed and hurried to join the girl at the table.

He'd been a means to an end.

Too bad he wanted more.

Much more.

The realization stopped him. Cold. It would never work. He had to distance himself from this kid before he forgot she was too young and his cynical self was no good for her.

"Are you joining us, Jack?" Her dimple appeared as she grinned, all worry about the league seeming to evaporate as she joined Dolly and her teammates at the table. "There's even a seat by me."

"No thanks. I'm not interested in being a fifth wheel." His pride couldn't handle it. A few of the Jewels batted eyelashes at him, and he reconsidered. What would it hurt? Jack grabbed the chair, flipped it around, and straddled it as Kat's eyebrows shot up.

"What are you doing?" she hissed.

"Accepting your invitation after all."

She turned her back on him and launched into an animated conversation with Dolly. After a few minutes of trying to follow their banter, he gave up and focused on the cutie next to him. He was the only man at the table, surrounded by women. Even if Kat avoided him the rest of the evening, he liked the odds. Jack reviewed the small menu. Looked like ethnic food—Slovenian—filled the options. Good thing he was ready to try something new.

"So what are you doing with her when you could be with me?" A brunette winked at him.

He wanted to laugh at her brashness but decided to play along. "I'm her ticket to break free."

The woman considered his words. The candles flickered, sending shadows flitting around the table. A waitress came along and took their orders.

"I can't understand why she's more interested in Dolly than you. Her loss."

"Dolly seems like a good kid."

The woman snorted, charm school forgotten or abandoned. "It'll take awhile for her to fit in with the team. I don't know why they decided to shift players at this point in the season. Not great for team unity."

"They're trying to keep the teams balanced."

"So they say."

The candles flickered again, and Kat stiffened next to him. "Oh no."

Jack turned to see what had her on edge. Joanie strode toward them, a grimace fixed on her face.

"Katherine Miller, you know the rules. There's no fraternizing with another team's members. Come with me."

Kat's chin jerked up, and he sensed her turmoil. Would she acquiesce or let the woman have it? He knew which he rooted for, but Kat didn't have it in her.

ten

Two more games, split between a win and a loss, and the Blossoms headed back to Cherry Hill. Not a moment too soon. Kat didn't know how much more of living under Joanie's microscope she could handle. If she'd understood how quickly one simple dinner would put her on Joanie's list, she might have followed the rules. Instead she now had to check in with Joanie first thing in the morning and clear all of her nonpractice and nongame activities.

But it had been worth it. She'd needed the time with a friend. Someone who cared about her and not about how she played that day.

Kat didn't think this string of games would ever end. She didn't want to spend another night trying to sleep on a train as the team traveled to the next city. Instead she'd end up watching one or two groups play cards, while another group belted out song after off-key song. Then they'd stagger from the train in Cherry Hill with one day to recover before hitting the grind again with home games—and that only if she didn't count the late-afternoon practice.

Her bed at the Harrisons' home was all she wanted. The privacy of a room, no matter how small, that she shared with no one and could close the door of sounded so wonderful she almost cried.

Yet another sign the stress of travel and the game schedule had hit home.

She tried to stifle a yawn that threatened to break her jaw.

"Come here, kid."

She looked down at Jack, his look inviting her to sit down even as his nickname grated. Joanie jumped to her feet, and

Kat shuffled forward. The leash had tightened since her escapade with Dolly. Why couldn't Jack find another car filled with new passengers to annoy rather than allow his presence to remind Joanie of Kat's transgressions?

"Good night, Jack." She whispered the words as she stumbled down the lurching car, settling in a vacant row. For once she wouldn't fight a losing battle with a dozen soldiers for a seat. Tucking her purse under her head, she curled up on the seats. Not as comfortable as her bed at home. She closed her eyes against sudden moisture. What she wouldn't give for one night at home, familiar food, and people who loved her for who she was, not what she did.

This was not the time to break down. Not where her teammates could watch. They didn't need ammunition reinforcing the fact she didn't have their level of sophistication. Some days she didn't want their maturity. Other times she wished for the hard shell some of them wore. Its protection worked for them.

A weight plopped in front of her, rocking the seat back. She prayed it wasn't Jack. No matter how much she pretended, he wasn't one of her brother's friends, someone she could pal around with and not wish for more. No, Jack had worked his way deeper.

Kat opened her eyes and relaxed when she caught Manager Addebary watching her. "Sir?"

"How you doing, kid?"

She pushed up to a sitting position, pulling on her A-Okay face. "I'm fine."

He studied her in a way that suggested he saw through her words. "I hope so. Anyway, I have news for you."

"You're shipping me home." She bit her lower lip to steel herself against tears.

"No. Not this time anyway. Too many escapades like you had with the Jewels and my hands might be tied." He held up his hand as she started to protest. "Listen, kid, I understand.

It's been lonely for you. But rules are rules.

"Anyway, we got the list for the all-star game next week at Wrigley. You're on the team. Just keep Joanie happy for a week, and you'll play. You might volunteer for the USO dance, too. You know how she feels about those."

"Yes sir." She rocked on the seat. "Can I tell anyone?"

"I'd wait until it's in the paper in the morning. No need for them to hear about it from you. Let others share the good news for you. Should keep things simpler around here." He pushed up. "I've got a few more to tell. Keep up the effort, Katherine."

Her eyes misted at the proud, paternal tone in his voice.

❧

Good for her. Jack wouldn't pretend that he hadn't overheard the news. Instead he enjoyed watching wonder fill Kat's eyes. She looked at him with a *who me?* shrug of her shoulders. Jack considered moving to the seat next to her and hugging her but kept his distance. She'd be embarrassed by the demonstration—even if he meant it in celebration

He winked at her and left it at that as soft color flooded her face.

She half turned away, as if to avoid seeing him, but not fast enough. Jack saw the grin and knew she enjoyed the mild flirting as much as the next girl. But since he'd met her in Chicago last month, there'd been no one else for him. He didn't even miss Polly, which felt a little odd after spending time with her most weeks since he'd arrived in Cherry Hill. Still, her appeal had dimmed in Kat's light. Kat fascinated him from the top of her curly head to the tips of her toes that knew how to slide into base as well as the next guy.

What a paradox.

And headed to the USO dance. Jack smiled. He couldn't wait to see Kat in that environment. Surrounded by red-blooded American men headed to one of the fronts. Should be a shock to her system. It was one thing to do a victory formation at each game. An entirely different thing to be hounded by men who might not see a woman for months. Okay, that was a slight exaggeration since these men hadn't shipped out yet.

The train slowed in jerks and starts. Jack rocked with the train and looked out the window. The northern Indiana landscape that surrounded Cherry Hill pulled into view. The town's grove of cherry trees looked wilted under the intense heat, but the leaves fluttered. He hoped the breeze would cool him once he stepped off the train.

A glance at his watch showed he had time to swing by his room before hurrying to the newspaper to write tomorrow's stories. Maybe that all-important letter from UPI waited.

He edged to the front of the car and detrained as soon as the last shudder swept through the cars. He tipped his hat at Kat and hurried down the platform toward the depot. As the sun blazed, Jack rolled up his shirtsleeves, juggling his satchel all the while.

By the time he reached his apartment, sweat rolled down his back. He'd need a shower before he worked his way to the office. His landlady had stacked his mail on the table as usual, and he grabbed it before collapsing on his bed. He flipped through the envelopes, stopping only when he found the one with the UPI logo. Tossing the rest of the mail on the floor, he ripped open the envelope.

Dear Mr. Raymond,

Thank you for your letter of inquiry. At this time we have no openings for reporters whose experience is focused on sports and women's sports at that. We wish you the best in your future endeavors.

Sincerely,
The Editors
United Press International

Jack crumpled up the letter.

The contents shouldn't surprise him. Why would a service like UPI take him seriously? He remained a small-town nobody covering a nonexistent sport. If things didn't change soon, he wouldn't even report on the league.

He needed to make something happen.

He wouldn't leave his destiny in the hands of anonymous men sitting in some high-rise in a big city. No, he'd do what he did best. Write stories that garnered their attention. The kind of stories that made them sit up and notice his skills. And he'd ask Ed for a new assignment. One that better positioned him to leave.

In a rush he cleaned up, changed, and headed to the *Cherry Hill Gazette*. If he was in luck, Ed would be there and he could tackle the last item on his list.

He winked at Doreen. "That's a smart outfit."

The woman blushed to the tips of her gray hair.

"Is Ed in?"

"Gulping an antacid. Be forewarned."

Jack patted her desk. "Thank you, ma'am." He strode across the newsroom to Ed's office. The door stood closed with the blinds drawn. Usually that signaled it was a good time to give Ed space. Right now Jack didn't care. He rapped on the door and opened it before Ed answered. He sauntered into the room and plopped into the chair in front of Ed's desk.

A fizzy glass bubbled on the corner of the battered desk. Ed had his back to the door, phone pinned by his shoulder against his ear. "Fine. Keep me updated." He spun around and slammed the phone down. "Bureaucrats." He looked at Jack. "What are you doing here?"

"Writing your lead article for tomorrow's paper."

Ed snorted. "Doubt that. You've got to give me more than these blow-by-blow accounts of the games." He rubbed his hands across his balding scalp. "We'll never fill the stands this way."

"I wanted to talk about that. How about running a contest?"

Jack laced his fingers and leaned forward. His mind raced as the idea came to him. "We could have a kiss-the-player contest. Sell war bonds in the process. A direct link to helping the war effort. More than the V formation and an occasional USO dance."

"How do you get the players to agree?"

"The typical spiel about doing their part for the war." Jack could even think of a player from whom he'd buy a war bond in order to kiss.

Ed cleared his throat. "I don't know."

"Marlene Dietrich and other stars have done it across the country. Why not our stars? Let's paint them as the stars we want them to be. More than hawking groceries for Bill's Market. Maybe it could be a campaign that culminates with the Cherry Hill Festival at the end of July."

"Maybe." Ed launched forward on the edge of his seat. "Put together a plan, and see if the players will agree."

"Done."

"And get me some articles I can use. More like those features on Faye and Katherine Miller. Readers ate those up."

Jack nodded. What else could he do? "I've got a few ideas from this last trip. Some day-in-the-life kind of things."

"I don't care what they are as long as they get people to the games. Get out of here."

"Yes, sir." Jack stood as Ed held his nose and picked up the bubbly drink. "Bottoms up."

Jack glanced at his watch and hustled to his desk. If he hurried, he could still make it to the USO dance. First he had to write the articles filling his mind.

❧

"Can I come in?" Victoria, the Harrisons' eight-year-old, waltzed into the room without waiting for an answer.

Kat turned from her vanity with a smile, amazed at how the child had grown on her since her arrival. "Whatcha up to, kiddo?"

Victoria rocked her foot back and forth, as if drawing a picture in a sand dune with her toes. "I wondered. Can I come with you tonight? To the dance?"

Kat bit her tongue to keep from laughing. "That would be fun, wouldn't it? I'm not much of a dancer. I bet you're better than me. But you're not old enough."

"I'll never be old enough to do anything." The child planted her hands on her hips, a perfect mirror for her mother's frustrated stance.

"I'm sorry. How about a special outing on my next free day? Just you and me."

"Really?" Victoria shrieked. "Get an ice cream. Maybe see a movie?"

"Victoria Rose Harrison. You do not invite yourself into Katherine's life. She's plenty busy without spending time with you." Mrs. Harrison sighed, an apology in her eyes. "I'm so sorry."

"I don't mind. Victoria is a delight."

The little girl stood straighter at the words. "See, Mama. She likes me." She skipped from the room, humming a tune.

"I appreciate the ways you help. Please don't feel obligated."

"I don't mind." Kat looked into the mirror, patted her cheeks, and frowned at the multiplying field of freckles. "Well, nothing I can do about these dots."

"No one notices them. Trust me. If they do, it's only because they enhance your looks."

"Yeah, the perpetually cute one."

Mrs. Harrison laughed, and the lines around her eyes eased. "You have plenty of time to find the man who captures your imagination. When you find him, you'll never let him go. Just look at us. When I met Wayne ten years ago, I never imagined I'd leave my home state or have four children in such short order." She turned to leave. "I'll leave you to your preparations."

"Do you ever regret it?"

"Regret what?" Mrs. Harrison leaned down to pick up Eric, their youngest.

Kat searched for the right words. "Regret getting married young? Following your husband to a new place?"

"No. It's challenged me at times, but that's okay." Eric whimpered, and she jostled him on her hip. "You need to finish dressing. Wear your emerald dress. I'll prepare a snack for you in the kitchen."

Kat turned back to the mirror. Her slip felt silky against her skin, a forgotten feeling after weeks of softball uniforms. She painted her legs with the leg cream—a necessity since hose had become impossible to find with rationing—then examined them. Almost as good as hose, though she doubted even that could cover all the bruises. She powdered then slipped on the emerald dress. Its simple lines settled over her as if it had been tailored for her, and the color brought extra attention to her eyes. The length of the dress didn't hurt anything either. She applied lipstick but avoided the other cosmetics. Even after the charm lessons she didn't feel comfortable using many of them. The sailors wouldn't care. She grabbed her purse and slipped from her room. After retrieving her snack from the kitchen, Kat went to the front porch. The shade kept the temperature bearable as she waited for her ride.

After a few minutes a car pulled up to the curb. Faye hopped out, beautiful in a navy dress with a gossamer scarf floating around her shoulders. "Ready, Kat?"

"Yes." Her voice quavered on the word. Why did this feel so important? She'd grown up around Mark's friends. But that had been in comfortable surroundings with no pressure. Tonight felt different.

Rosie and Lola waited in the car. Kat tried to stifle her reaction to Lola's shocking, heavy makeup.

Lola smacked her gum and examined Kat. "I guess I was wrong. You actually are coming. You'll have a good time with the boys."

Kat hoped so but had doubts. She couldn't be further out of her league if she tried. She almost said something then decided Lola wouldn't understand that she wanted a man who understood how to promise her forever.

eleven

A swing band played radio favorites from a dais at the front of the room. The packed bodies had heated the ballroom long before Jack waltzed into the room. He tugged down his sleeve cuffs and entered the fray. He didn't care about the crush, the sailor and military uniforms mixing with a sea of colorful dresses. He wanted to find one person.

See if Miss Katherine Miller relaxed in an environment like this.

It had to be a far cry from the high school dances she might have attended in Dayton. He doubted she'd done that. She seemed the type to alternate between studying, playing ball, and drills.

But even Katherine needed an opportunity to relax, let down her hair, enjoy the moment.

As long as he shared the moment. The guys outnumbered the gals two to one, leaving a tight sensation in his gut—something he'd never experienced with Polly. Jack didn't want to imagine any number of these men pawing Kat. Would she even know what to do? Playing with guys on the field was different from this scene. She needed someone to step in and protect her. Whether she knew it or not.

He scanned the room, looking for the spitfire. She stood against a wall, surrounded by sailors. Although the lines of her body suggested she was relaxed and enjoying the attention, Jack detected a small furrow between her eyes, the one that only appeared when she felt outmaneuvered. Faye danced by on the arm of a grunt, while Lola swayed entirely too close with an officer of some sort. It looked like GI Joes had grabbed all of Kat's teammates, leaving her to fend for herself.

Would he be a hero or a dog if he stepped in and swept her onto the dance floor?

Her laugh, soft and hesitant, reached his ears. That settled it; he couldn't leave her alone, not with those men.

Jack ambled toward the group, clearing his throat when he reached it. "Miss Miller, you look radiant tonight. You promised to save a spot for me on your dance card."

A spark filled her eyes. "Why, Mr. Raymond, I wondered if you'd stood me up. I would like that dance very much." She turned to the boys around her, a lilt in her voice as she played along. "If you'll excuse me. I'll look for you later."

"If she has time." Jack extended his hand and relaxed when her small hand slipped into his. How did she manage to snag so many balls with hands that delicate?

"You can't keep her to yourself, bud." A soldier thrust his chest out and took a step toward Jack.

"I hear you. We'll leave it up to her." He turned Kat toward the dance floor and away from the men.

"You are a welcome sight in this sea of strangers." Kat edged closer to him as they squeezed through the crowd. "Could we go outside rather than dance?"

"Don't you know how?" He'd meant it as a tease but, at her silence, realized she really might not have any moves. "Charleston? Jitterbug? Waltz?" She shook her head as he ticked through several additional styles of dancing. "Well, I'll teach you at least the waltz. Everyone needs to dance a waltz or two at a wedding or anniversary celebration."

As they talked, he eased her toward the door. He pushed through one side of the double-glass doors, breathing deeply of the fresh air that didn't feel so stifling in comparison to the hall. Notes of a clarinet wailing a Tommy Dorsey tune filtered from an open window. Kat cocked her head as if wanting to absorb every note.

"Isn't that beautiful?"

The saxophone shrieked a sour note, and Jack rubbed the

back of his neck and winced. "If you like your beauty with a big side of melancholy and squeak."

Kat laughed. "Thank you again for rescuing me."

"My pleasure." Jack studied her a moment, until he knew his only options were to turn away or kiss her. He turned.

Twilight shadowed the cityscape as he walked Kat toward his car. He leaned against it and studied the sky.

"What are you doing?" Her breath tickled his ear as she settled next to him.

He took a steadying breath, keeping his gaze locked on the sky. "Waiting for the first evening star."

Silence followed, broken only by the rustle of leaves as the breeze brushed through the trees. Would she say anything? Most women fidgeted at the first moment of stillness. Yet Kat seemed to absorb the peace, unhurried.

Mercifully the song ended, and the band leader announced a break. The pop and hiss of a record took the place of the saxophone. As the easy three-four time of a waltz slipped through the open windows, Jack stood. "May I have this dance?"

Kat considered him, a slight tension squeezing her shoulders. After a moment she nodded her head and stood. He slipped his right hand around her waist, sensing the catch in Kat's breathing as he did. He took her right hand in his left and eased into the three-step waltz. "One, two, three. One, two, three." He crooned the words in time with the music. "Do you feel the rhythm?"

She nodded, and he looked down at her. Her lower lip was caught between her teeth, and her steps stuttered a half count behind each of his.

"One, two, three. One, two, three." She'd settle down as she felt the music. Everyone did.

A tremor vibrated up Kat's spine. Jack looked down at her again and slowed. "Are you okay, Kat?"

If she bit her lip any harder, blood would stain her glossed lips.

"Katherine Miller, are you out here?" Joanie's high-pitched whine pierced the darkness. Kat jumped in his arms, putting space between them. "I see you, young lady. You're here to dance with the boys, and certainly not alone with a man."

She tugged her hand free and pushed away. "I–I'm sorry. I can't do this."

Before he could say anything, probe for a reason beyond Joanie's sudden appearance, Kat turned and fled into the building.

He took a deep breath, the warmth of her body lingering in the empty space.

Katherine Miller was nothing more than a child. Her flight proved that fact. Yet he had never felt the way he did about her. He wanted to prolong their interactions but had to admit it had nothing to do with the fact she served as the subject for his ongoing reports on the Blossoms.

No, it had everything to do with the fact Katherine Miller was a woman. She might not realize it yet, but everyone else did. And he couldn't imagine watching her with anyone else.

❧

All week, softballs roiled in Kat's stomach. She couldn't seem to avoid Joanie's censoring or Jack's presence. When she'd headed outside with Jack, it had never occurred to her that Joanie would add it to her list of wrongs. Her request to step outside had seemed like a simple solution to avoiding Joanie. She couldn't have been more wrong. And she was flummoxed about how to change Joanie's view of her. Nothing wrong had happened with Jack.

Every time she caught Jack watching her, she flushed as hot as a Sunday afternoon at the hint of promise and desire in his eyes. That had never appeared in the eyes of any of the high school boys.

Maybe nothing had happened at the dance, but part of her wondered what might have if Joanie hadn't appeared. All Jack had wanted to do was teach her to dance. So why had she felt so vulnerable through each word murmured in her ear and every second his hand touched her waist? She tried to tell herself Jack was simply another of Mark's friends, but her heart refused to accept the words.

In the end, Addebary sent her to the all-star game over Joanie's objections. Said it would be good for the team. But the uptight looks and cold shoulders her teammates sent her way left Kat wondering if the team wouldn't be better served by Faye going to the game instead of her.

The calendar read July 1. Another hotel. Another day. Another city. This time Chicago.

Tonight she would play in Wrigley Field.

Kat rolled over then grimaced as she shifted across her latest strawberry. Just once, she wished she could slide into base without destroying her thigh. At this rate she'd have permanent black, purple, and yellow blotches long after the season ended.

An all-star. The idea seemed preposterous. So many Blossoms played as hard or better than she. But she'd been selected thanks to Jack's articles that a wire service had picked up. She didn't want to think popularity rather than skill had led to her selection, but. . . .

Come on, Kat. Just accept it as an honor and enjoy the experience. She could hear her mother's advice as if the woman sat on the bed next to her. Sound advice, as always. Yet so hard to implement.

Whatever the reason she'd been chosen, she'd play shortstop for one of the teams. Maybe the stands would be full. Even if they weren't, she'd still play in Wrigley Field, something girls simply didn't do.

This was an honor. One she should enjoy to the maximum.

Soon enough the game would end, and tomorrow she'd rejoin her teammates in South Bend. Back to the grind of games, doubleheaders, travel, and more games. It might be July 1, but it felt like the season had already lasted much longer than one month.

Surely Jack hadn't made the trip.

Her heart skipped at the thought.

It shouldn't matter whether he had. She longed for one friendly face. One person to reassure her she belonged here. That it wasn't a fluke her name made the list. A pain shot through her. She couldn't look to Jack for those assurances.

Father, I'm sorry. I want You to be my source of security. I've done such a lousy job lately of keeping You in my thoughts. Tears pricked her eyes then slid down her cheeks. She swiped at them with the coarse comforter she had wrapped around herself. *Be my security. Help me find my identity in You and not in those around me.*

She wanted to be a light for Him but felt like such a failure. It seemed no matter how hard she tried, her efforts only made things worse.

Today she was Joanie-less, since a different chaperone had made the trip to Chicago. For today she didn't have to worry about how her every action and intention might be misinterpreted. She should focus on that, enjoy the momentary freedom. And revel in why she was here.

Wrigley Field.

Kat glanced at the bedside alarm clock and jumped out of bed. If she didn't hurry, she'd miss the press lunch. Then practice and the game. In no time the day would be behind her.

She pulled on her Blossoms uniform and hurried to the lobby. The concierge gave her directions to the luncheon. She thanked him and turned to leave. A familiar face peered at her over the top of a newspaper. Jack stood with a lazy smile and ambled over to her.

"Ready for the big day?"

Kat pressed a hand on her stomach. She opened her mouth, but nothing came out.

"Don't worry. You'll be great."

"The press will have me for lunch."

"You'll have them following you around like love-struck kids by the end of the hour."

A shudder shook through her at the thought. "You mean they'll all be like you?" She clapped a hand over her mouth. "I'm sorry."

Jack grimaced then put an arm around her shoulders. "You might want to watch the comments like that. I understand that arrow, which pierced my poor, vulnerable heart." She rolled her eyes, and he laughed. "But the press here in the Windy City is more. . .cut-throat. They'll gladly take any information you give them and twist it." He gestured like a knife had plunged into her heart.

"You certainly know how to encourage a person." She slipped from his arm and put space between them. Jack kept pushing under her guard, something she couldn't allow. At the end of the summer she had to go home and finish school, and he couldn't be truly interested in a high school senior. Not when he could have any woman he wanted. Certainly any number of her teammates would take him on as a charity case.

And she still wasn't sure about his faith. If he had ever had any, something had turned him highly cynical.

She couldn't imagine sharing forever with someone who didn't value his relationship with God as much as she valued hers.

Her breath caught in her chest.

Forever?

❧

Jack straightened his fedora and edged into the stands. Fans sat around Wrigley Field, but the stands weren't full. He could stretch out and take a nap without fear of someone brushing by him. Still, there were more spectators than at any game he'd covered so far. The smell of hot, buttered popcorn made his stomach growl. He massaged his forehead, the remnants of last night's outing with college buddies pulsing in his temples. His stomach might think it needed food, but he knew the first bite would have him running for the facilities.

A cheer erupted from the stands as the women streamed out of the dugouts. They wore standard skirts—white for one team and yellow for the other—but the blouses came from their regular team uniforms. They formed a sherbet-colored rainbow.

Real ballplayers didn't wear pastels.

He must be hungover.

It had been awhile since he'd felt that way about the AAGPBL. He pulled a program out of his pocket. Kat's friend Dolly had made the same all-star team. He imagined the two having a great time for the day they'd be together.

Although the idea of an all-star game sounded great, the reality was brutal for the players. Their teammates had a day off, but the all-stars had traveled to Chicago, would play the game, and then rejoin their teammates in time for the next game.

The announcer introduced the players, his voice crackling over the public address system. Kat stepped forward with a big grin and wave when he announced her name. Her steps bounced, and energy radiated from her.

His star.

Jack settled in, waiting for the moment she would snag the ball or make the play that solidified her stature in the game.

She might be seventeen, but that wasn't too young—just look at fifteen-year-old Dottie Schrader, who had locked in her place in the league's history books. Time for everyone outside Cherry Hill to realize that Katherine Miller had the same playing ability and star quality.

The first six innings had Jack fighting to pay attention. The play inched along, with the focus being the contest between the pitcher and batter. The powers-that-be should have selected Faye Donahue for one of the teams. She at least would have been easy on the eyes while time faded.

During the seventh-inning stretch Jack jerked to attention.

"My special guest today is Miss Katherine Miller," the announcer spit into the microphone. "What are you here to tell us about, little lady?"

Jack laughed, drawing curious stares from the few people seated around him. "She hates to be called that."

"It's all about war bonds." Kat's voice sounded honey-dipped, so much so he could imagine the furrow between her brows. "Today the players have agreed to sign autographs for those who buy a war bond."

"One war bond equals one autographed picture?"

"Yes, sir."

"So if a fan wants everyone's photo?"

"That's more than twenty war bonds, and the buyer's a real patriot."

"For that many, I'd think people would expect more than photos."

Jack cocked his head, wanting to catch her reply.

There was a slight pause. Had her mouth fallen open in shock? Was she considering slapping the guy? Jack rubbed his jaw, imagining the impact.

"Well, sir, what exactly do you have in mind?"

The man cleared his throat, and Jack smiled at his discomfort.

"I'm not sure what's going through your mind, sir, but this is America's wholesome pastime. We're delighted to provide a great example to younger girls who hope to someday play ball themselves. So the players will be happy to sign one photo for each war bond."

"Yes!" Jack pumped his fist in the air.

Kat's quote would lead all the articles about the all-star game. His star had just grown.

twelve

The train rocked from side to side as it raced to Kenosha, Wisconsin. The Blossoms had started the second half of the season on fire. Did it have something to do with the fans filling the seats at games? It seemed that in every town they played, enthusiasm for the league had improved. Even in Cherry Hill the stands had reached capacity a time or two.

Now the Blossoms must find a rhythm that led to the playoffs. To do that, they needed to at least split the series, or their season might as well be over.

The longer Kat played with the Blossoms, the more life evolved into something complicated. And the more the thought of her final year of school welcomed her. She knew what to expect there. The role to play. Here nothing made sense anymore. Everything sucked the energy from her as she tried to please all those around her and failed miserably.

There's only One you need to please.

The words whispered through her soul. But how could she honor everyone while focusing on Him?

"It would be easier if everyone else served You."

Addebary stumbled up the aisle, and she looked away. Maybe he'd go somewhere else. She didn't have the energy to pretend right now.

"Kat Miller. You had a great series, kid."

"Thanks, sir." Kat glanced across the car and caught Rosie staring at her, frown lines etched into the grooves of her face.

"You're coming back next year, aren't you?"

Kat shrugged. "Probably. But we'll have to see how school goes. My parents are pretty keen on me finishing and looking at college."

The man rubbed his paunch and nodded. "Understood.

Keep playing like you have the last few weeks, and you'll have a spot on any team. With the stadiums filled, they're expanding the league. They'll need even more players to fill all the spots."

"I'll pray about it."

"That's all I ask, kid. I'd love to have you back. Well. . ." He launched to his feet. "I'm headed to the dining car for some food. Need anything?"

"No, thank you."

After he left, Kat pulled out a paperback. She didn't know much about the book, but it had been inexpensive at the station's newsstand. She'd barely turned to page 4 when someone plopped down next to her.

"You are something else, you know that?" Lola crossed her arms and glared at Kat.

Kat wrinkled her forehead, trying to figure out what Lola meant.

"You know that double play from the other day?" Kat nodded. "Guess who got all the credit for it? Yep, your boyfriend made it out like you whizzed around the field getting both outs. Must be nice to have someone color the world rosy for you."

"I don't understand."

"Guess what. I'm tired of the innocent act. It doesn't do a thing for me anymore. You're working the angles like the rest of us. Only thing is, you get all the breaks. The good press. The all-star game. Not content to leave any crumbs for the rest of us. Not that I want your crumbs."

Kat fought the surge of heat that colored her vision. She should let Lola's words go. Turn the other cheek. But she couldn't. Not anymore. "I have done nothing to you. I haven't asked for any of this. Faye should have been at the all-star game. Not me."

"You've got that right."

"But guess what? I wasn't the one making the selection. I

just went where they sent me. Like I do every day." People turned toward them. She needed to lower her voice, but it was like a valve had been released. She couldn't stop herself.

"I never asked for the newspaper coverage either. All I want to do is play ball. That's it. I'd love to make a few friends, but that doesn't even seem possible. So excuse me if life isn't the way you wanted it or imagined it. But it hasn't turned out that way for me either." Kat stood then stumbled as the train swayed. Her gaze locked with Jack's. Her cheeks flamed. When had he entered the car? It didn't matter. His gaze searched her with a knowing expression. She had to get away and protect herself from him. Kat grabbed her purse and ran.

❧

Jack watched Kat go. Listening to her, a flare shot through him.

She deserved better.

Son, never fail to treat others the way you'd choose to be treated. His mother's words echoed through his heart. She wouldn't understand his need to do whatever it took to climb to a better paper in a bigger city. Instead, if he bothered to ask, she'd probably tell him to do right and trust the Lord to handle the details.

Those words used to make so much sense.

Then the world fell apart, and he'd struggled to find his footing ever since.

Maybe that was the crux of the issue. He'd struggled. Maybe he needed to step back and trust again the One who had planned his life long before he drew his first breath.

He'd have to think some more on that. But right now he needed to apologize for the way he'd set up Kat. Although he hadn't foreseen the way the other players would react, he hadn't changed anything once he became aware of their attitudes either. And he wouldn't want to be treated that way.

Sure, he hadn't done anything intentional. Who wouldn't like starring in the articles? But he'd never stopped to ask her.

He'd rolled over her like everyone else.

He needed to follow her, but glue must have adhered to the seat of his pants. Rosie looked at him with a glint in her eyes.

"Can't do it, can you?"

"Huh?" He'd play dumb. Nobody else needed to know his thoughts.

"Remorse is a terrible thing."

"Don't know what you mean."

"Hmm." She looked at him, a calculating set to her face. "Isn't she a bit young for you? There are plenty of women on the team. You don't have to settle for a kid. She's sweet, but that's not what you want."

Her words wove around his mind, a glaring counterpoint to the direction his thoughts had just taken. He needed to leave. Get out of Dodge.

"I know someone who's interested, but not while you moon over a kid. So if you're ready for a real woman. . ."

A warning screamed in his mind. He needed to get away from Rosie before he acted on her offer. "Let her know I'm not interested now. Life's too busy."

That had to be the weakest excuse he'd come up with in a long time, but it gave him the gumption he needed to move. He hightailed it out of the railcar before her siren call wove an unbreakable spell.

A moment later he entered the dining car and froze. Kat huddled at a corner table. He hesitated. She was a kid. But that didn't change the truth. He wanted to be with her but couldn't let himself. Before she could see him, he turned and hotfooted out of there like a coward.

❧

Kat tugged her suitcase into a Kenosha hotel lobby. This one didn't look so different from the others she'd walked into this summer. Faded carpet, a couple of stuffed chairs, bored desk attendant. Kat accepted her room key from Joanie, found the room, and deposited her suitcase. Then she joined the rest of the team on the walk to the ball field. She strolled next to Faye but stayed silent as she listened to the chatter around her. Many of the gals talked about the dates they'd had during their last quick stay in Cherry Hill. Kat didn't have anything to add to that conversation. Most of the time she was glad, but today, for some reason, it left her feeling hollow.

They reached the clubhouse and changed into their practice uniforms before grabbing their gear.

"You with us, Kat?" Manager Addebary stared at her as if waiting for her to blow over in a stiff breeze.

"Yes, sir." Tired as she was, she'd do what it took to help the team. Since the all-star game, little risk remained of being sent home before the end of the season. Unless her stamina gave out.

"Then get out there."

Kat hurried to her position.

"If it isn't the princess." Lola chomped on a wad of gum. Kat tried to keep her gaze straight ahead and avoid the thought that Lola chewed like a cow on cud.

Rosie snickered. "Glad you could join us."

"Too bad some of your swarming fans didn't make the trip."

Kat tightened her jaw against the words she wanted to spout back. She wanted to play her best for whoever showed up to watch. And that required focused practice. "I'd really like to get ready for tonight."

"Oh, is that a command? Having money wasn't enough for you? You have to command the rest of us while you're here?" The hard edge to Lola's voice brought Kat up short. What was the story? Something had to make the woman so hateful.

Kat opened her mouth then closed it. Someone had to be the adult and do the mature thing. And that meant letting Lola's words go. *Lord, help me bite my tongue and give me abundant grace for Lola and Rosie. Please.*

"Shouldn't you gals warm up something other than your mouths?"

Not that annoying, wonderful voice. If she wasn't careful, Jack would finish the transformation into the knight sent to defend her. Her heart tripped at the image of him vanquishing her foes and freeing her from their torment.

"If it isn't Jack Raymond. Defender of all helpless, underage maidens." Rosie rolled her eyes. "Don't forget there are real women out here."

Heat flashed through Kat at the blatant invitation in Rosie's words. How could someone be that brazen? In public?

"Miss Miller, could I have a moment of your time?" Kat had to shield her face to see the tight lines around Jack's eyes.

"What do you need, Jack?" She turned her most syrupy smile his way while trying to avoid eye contact. She did not need the jolt of looking into his eyes and the following confusion. She was too tired today to get her heart to cooperate.

"A quote from Cherry Hill's favorite softball player."

"Then you're in the wrong place. We're baseball players now."

"That's just a name change."

"Don't reporters pride themselves on getting the facts right?"

"Touché." Jack pushed off his bleacher and hiked down the stairs till he stood three or four rows above her. The annoying man forced her to keep her eyes shielded from the sun. "I still need that quote."

"And I need to get back to practice, or Cherry Hill's most popular player will lose her contract. If you'll excuse me." Kat took a step back.

"Duck!"

Kat turned around in time to see the softball blazing toward her. Then everything went black.

❧

"Come on, kid."

Why was something tickling her neck? Kat tried to move but stopped as pain pulsed through her head. Was she lying down? That didn't make sense. And why was someone slapping her cheeks? Kat held a hand to her head. "Stop." She'd meant the word to be forceful, but it trickled out in a whisper.

"You took a softball to the head." Jack's voice came from overhead. Did his breath brush her cheek? She tried to open her eyes, but the lids felt so heavy. Too heavy. Instead she rested.

"Katherine Miller. What have you done now?" Joanie clucked her tongue. "And I thought strawberries were painful. Looks like you'll have a goose egg before that swelling stops. Someone get some ice for the girl's head."

A murmuring in the background built until it sounded like a swarm of mosquitoes.

Kat licked her lips. "Could you tell everyone the show's over?"

"Hmm? All right, gang. Back to practice." Addebary shouted instructions, and soon Kat felt movement vibrate through the ground.

"Here, this will feel cold." Joanie thrust something frigid against her hair. "We'll hold it in place for a while. Give the bruising a chance to ease. Do you think you can sit up?"

"I can try." Kat screwed her eyes shut as someone tugged on each arm, pulling her upright. Gingerly she eased one eye and then the other open. The world didn't shift, but a headache pounded from the egg at the back of her head.

"You won't play tonight, but it looks like you'll live."

"Thanks, Joanie." It wouldn't be the last time a ball beaned her, but Kat appreciated seeing the softer side of the chaperone. The side that cared more about the players than enforcing all the rules.

"I'll call a cab for you. No need for you to wait here while everyone else practices."

"I'll get her there."

Joanie eyed Jack, clearly skeptical and with a hint of

mama-bear protectiveness. Maybe she really just wanted to shield Kat, and that explained her strictness. Then Joanie looked at the field. "I guess that would work this once. Don't try anything funny."

He looked at Joanie with an innocent expression that said, "Who me?" Kat would have laughed if she hadn't feared it would hurt.

"Really, I'm fine."

"Sure you are, kid. Let's get you on your feet." He hauled her up, and she closed her eyes against the sudden swaying sensation. "Yeah, I'd say you're ready to get around by yourself. Come on."

Kat leaned against Jack and opened her eyes long enough to catch the uncertainty in Joanie's eyes. Maybe the woman wasn't so hard after all. Just unsure how to best protect her charges.

"Remember, no men in your room."

thirteen

The article Jack wrote about the series of Kenosha games highlighted Kat's ball to the head yet somehow managed to make her look heroic.

He thought she'd thank him. Instead she'd avoided him. So much for his good intentions. He didn't understand women. That couldn't be clearer.

But as the team crept back into Cherry Hill early Monday morning, a surprise awaited them. Fans packed the train station's platform.

"Way to go, girls!"

"Win some while you're home."

"Glad to see you're okay, Kat."

The appearance of a hundred or more fans seemed to jolt the team. Faye grinned and waved as if she'd morphed into Marlene Dietrich. Rosie sidled to the side and disappeared into the arms of a waiting plant worker. Kat looked at Jack, a befuddled expression on her adorable face.

He leaned in next to her. "I think they want a speech."

"Then they'll have to wait for Addebary."

"He doesn't seem like the speech type."

"Neither am I. Good day, Mr. Raymond." Before he could stop her, Kat slipped from his side and through the crowd, stopping periodically to sign a program or other piece of paper some fan thrust in her face. She seemed to do so with good humor but a touch of speed. Then she disappeared.

The middle of July had arrived and with it a shortening season. It wouldn't be too many more weeks before the season ended, most of the girls leaving with it. That didn't bother him until he thought of one player.

He needed to maximize his time with her. Jack hurried after Kat. She couldn't have gotten too far. He stopped when he spotted her half a block from the depot. A young man stood in front of her, blocking her path, but she didn't seem to mind. Jack picked up his pace, in case she needed his help.

"We've—I've missed you at church."

Kat shrugged. "I can't help it when a game takes us out of town."

The kid shuffled his feet. "I guess I'm trying to say. . . ." He cleared his throat. "I'd like to see you, if it's all right. Outside of church, I mean."

"Oh." The word popped out, and she clamped a hand over her mouth. It would be cute, if Jack didn't want to wring the neck of the acne-covered kid in front of her. "I'd enjoy that. If we can find time."

"Tonight? Dinner at Mary's Diner. Maybe a movie after that?"

Jack groaned. Tonight was a rare break for the Blossoms. Maybe he'd have to find a way to tag along. Make sure Kat was okay.

"I'd enjoy dinner but have to talk to the chaperone first." Kat took a step back. "I need to get home. It'll be a short night and practice comes early."

"I'll stop by at six, see if it's okay?"

Kat shrugged. "I'll look for you then." She hurried past him, her satchel thrown over her shoulder. The kid couldn't even stop and help her with her luggage. What a hero.

❧

Kat's mind spun as practice came to an end. Larry Chalmers had invited her to dinner, and Joanie had approved it. Part of her had a jumpy feeling, while the other part wanted to hide somewhere. He seemed nice, but uncertainty floated through her. "Anyone want to field some balls with me?"

Lola laughed at her. "Practice is over, kid."

Kat longed to tell Lola she'd never get better without the

extra practice, but it was clear anything she said would be ignored. Besides, she desperately needed the distraction while her mind wrestled with Larry.

"I'll stay." Kat looked up to see Annalise Fairchild stepping toward her. "I could use the extra work." A wistful tone touched her voice. The newcomer to the team in a trade that week, maybe she felt as lonely as Kat.

"Thank you."

The two pitched a ball back and forth, taking a step back each time they caught it until someone dropped the ball. Then they'd start all over again. As they worked, Kat teased the pertinent information from Annalise. An only child, her first foray out from under her parents' protective care came when she joined the league. She loved the experience but seemed jarred by the abrupt move.

"One morning I was a Peach, the next a Blossom." She sighed. "I really enjoyed Rockford."

"You'll like Cherry Hill, too, if you give it a little time."

"It's easy to see why you like it." Annalise rolled a ground ball her way.

Kat shuffled to the side and leaned over to capture it in her glove. "What do you mean?"

"A certain very handsome reporter has his eye on you. If I had someone like that watching me all the time, I'd think the town special, too."

Kat crossed her arms, stance firm as she stared at Annalise. "You're joshing."

"And I think you protest too much."

"Jack's older than my brother!"

"Jack?" Annalise crouched to field a ball. "Then you are close. Tell me you never had a crush on one of your brother's friends?" Annalise's chin lifted as if daring Kat to deny it. Something she couldn't do.

"There was Jason Summers."

"See." A delighted grin played on the girl's oval face. "Jack seems like a nice guy."

"He delights in teasing me."

"A sure sign of affection."

"Fine if you're a puppy." Kat tossed the ball hard. "I'm not. I want to be treated like a woman."

"Then start acting like one, rather than everybody's kid sister."

"It's what I am."

"But not the way to convince him you're a woman worthy of his love."

Kat wondered if she should smack her head. Why was she in the middle of a conversation like this?

"Come on, Kat. A man won't watch every hour of your practice and all your games if he doesn't care about you. They simply don't do that."

"I'm his assignment. And even if you're right, then he sees me as one of the guys. That always happens."

"Maybe back home, wherever that is."

"Dayton."

"Maybe in Dayton where they're used to having you around, but not Jack. He's only known you this summer. No images of a girl in pigtails to clutter his mind."

Kat tugged at a curl that had slipped out of her baseball cap. Maybe cutting her hair before the summer started had been a better idea than she'd originally thought. Otherwise she would have spent the last couple of months exactly as Annalise described.

Annalise laughed, the bell-like sound fresh. "You didn't."

"What?" Kat thought she pulled off the innocence.

"Wear pigtails? No wonder Jason whatever-his-name-was didn't notice you. Maybe you're the reason we had charm school." Annalise stood. "Well, time for this girl to get back to her room."

Annalise traipsed to the clubhouse, leaving Kat in a whirl of emotions that collided inside her. Could Jack really look at her that way? Did he have an interest in her that extended beyond being good story material?

Kat hurried to the clubhouse, grabbed her gear, and headed to her host home. The family was gone for the week; the quiet was exactly what she needed.

Jack was too old for her. She could imagine her parents' reaction if she came home with a serious relationship. Daddy would never let her leave the house again. In fact he might tutor her through the final year of school.

The image of sitting in a corner of her father's university office for a year made her laugh. The room overflowed with books, and if one fell, the rest would topple on top of her. She'd be buried alive and lucky if anyone found her before she turned into a skeleton. Kat's steps slowed when she reached the Harrisons' block. Some man sat on the front steps, elbows resting on his knees. She squinted against the sun, which formed a halo around him and silhouetted his features.

Kat hesitated. Should she proceed or go somewhere and wait until whoever this was disappeared?

"Larry." How could she forget he'd be there in fifteen minutes to pick her up? She squared her shoulders and marched toward the home. Whoever it was would have to get out of the way. She had a lot of work to do to get ready for an evening out.

Her steps slowed when the man stood. His features came into focus as Jack stepped toward her. "Afternoon, Kat."

"Jack." He'd never come to her home before. Why now? "What are you doing?"

"I thought you might like to join me for dinner." A smile tugged the corner of his mouth, giving him a William Holden air. His smile grew, as if he could read her thoughts.

Heat flashed across her cheeks. Why did she have to have her mother's porcelain skin?

"Come with me. Let's go have some fun. Relax a bit." Jack

waggled his eyebrows. "All work and no play make Katherine Miller a very dull girl."

She pulled her gaze from his lips and shook her head. "I've already got plans for tonight."

"What? Dinner with one your teammates? You don't seem to enjoy their company that much." He took another step toward her, and her breath hitched.

"No. A young man is calling for me soon." Kat took a step off the sidewalk to get around him. She had to get away from Jack before the combination of Annalise's words, her imagination, and his presence did her in. Her imagination wanted to fly away with her, picture what it would be like in his arms, but she couldn't let it.

Jack stepped in her path. The intensity in his eyes stole her thoughts. "Kat Miller, has anyone told you that you are an incredible woman?"

Woman? Had he just called her a woman? Not a kid? Not a tagalong? A woman?

She shook her head, trying to loosen her suddenly frozen words.

Another step closer to her. Her breath hitched again, and she forced her lungs to expand.

"You are. And I want to show you that tonight."

Wait a minute. What did that mean?

Kat shook her head and stepped back. "I have a date." With a nice, safe, young man. At least Larry seemed safe, especially when compared to Jack, who looked like he wanted to eat her for dessert. Maybe those times pitching a ball back and forth hadn't been so smart after all. Did he think she'd do anything for him?

"I have to go. Larry will arrive any moment. Excuse me." Kat slipped past him but was spun around.

"You can't go without this." A fire burned in Jack's eyes. Something shifted inside Kat as if he really did look into her and see her as more than she could see in herself. She suddenly felt beautiful and desirable. . .as a woman. The thought sucked her mouth dry.

Jack placed his hands on her waist and studied her face. Time froze in place as Kat wondered what Jack was thinking. She didn't dare ask him, certain she'd be shocked by his answer.

He lowered his mouth until it landed on top of hers. She stayed stiff for a moment then melted against him.

What are you doing?

A simple thought, but it had the effect of a bucket of ice water thrown on her. She gasped and pushed away from Jack. "You. . .can't."

Jack licked his lips, not letting go of her.

"Kat, is that you?"

She didn't want to look back and see Larry standing there. What must he think, seeing her like this? There was no way to explain this away.

Jack's dazed look quickly slid into his usual arrogant mask. "Are you sure you want to keep your plans with that kid when you could have me?"

She nodded. Anything had to be safer than spending time with Jack. The world felt tilted on its axis. She pushed away from Jack; this time he let her step back. She turned to Larry. "Give me a minute to get ready."

"All right." He hesitated, his gaze questioning her. "I'll—I'll wait here."

Kat hurried into the house then leaned against the door, cheeks blazing. She would go out with the safe option while her heart yearned for time with Jack. She had to get out of Cherry Hill. Soon.

fourteen

Another day, another train, this time to South Bend. Kat felt like she'd fallen from the train and rolled over a few times. Her muscles screamed for relief as she lay on top of the scratchy comforter on her hotel bed.

A knock came at the room's door. Kat rolled onto the floor and between the beds. "Yes?"

"There's a party waiting for you in the lobby, Miss Miller."

A party? Kat couldn't imagine who would seek her out in South Bend. "Thank you. I'll be down in a bit." Whoever it was would have to wait until she freshened up and dressed.

She considered climbing back onto the bed and ignoring whoever waited. In the end, she couldn't do it.

After a shower and quick application of approved cosmetics, Kat hurried to the elevator. Mirrors lined the walls, and she grimaced at her reflection as she stepped into the car. Even powder couldn't hide the purple smudges under her eyes. She had to find a better way to get sleep when traveling. Her mother would be horrified to see her like this.

The elevator doors slid open, and Kat stepped out. She scanned the lobby, curious to learn who waited.

"Katherine Miller, come over here."

A squeal bubbled through Kat at her mother's voice. She located her parents across the lobby and ran over. "Mama!"

Before she could do anything, Daddy engulfed her in a bear hug that pressed her face against his seersucker jacket. She inhaled the familiar musky scent that meant safety and love.

"Let me hug on her." Mama edged closer. She held Kat by the shoulders and studied her as if memorizing her face.

"Honey, what have they done to you?"

"Let me play softball—I mean, baseball."

Mama patted her cheeks. "We'll see if we can't get you some rest then. Come here." She led Kat to a couch. The lobby had seen better days, but Kat wanted to savor every unexpected moment with her family, as Joanie sat in a corner of the lobby, her eagle eyes trained on Kat. Again.

Kat sighed, wishing she understood the woman's antagonism. Someday she'd get to the bottom of it, but right now she wanted to spend the time with her parents. "Could we walk instead? Get some fresh air. I can't believe you're here."

"We wanted to slip up and surprise you. We drove up last night with the rest of the family. We left them at our hotel so we could see you first. You know how Cassandra will shadow you." Kat smiled at the reference to the girl from England whom her older sister, Josie, had taken in.

Daddy opened the door, and Kat let the tension bleed from her as she stepped into the sunlight. "They all came with you?"

"We felt bad about missing the all-star game, but it was too far. South Bend, however, was the ticket. Mark managed to slip away, so here we are."

Kat hugged her mother. The bone-deep loneliness eased in that embrace. Kat nestled against her mother and soaked in the moment.

"Are you all right, Kat?" Daddy's rich voice soothed her as surely as if he were holding her like he used to when she was a girl curled up on his lap, listening to him read.

"I'm so much better now that you're here."

"Your last postcards sounded down." Mama stroked her hair, a movement that had eased Kat's anxiety since she was a toddler.

"I'm all right." Her mother's look forced the truth from her. "The constant movement and lack of a real home tires me. But I'm okay. It's only for a season."

"And when you're invited back for next year?"

"That's already happened. Maybe I want to spend the summer after graduation in a different way." The August sun felt hot, so hot that even the birds stayed silent in their trees. Kat turned the corner so they could loop back to the hotel. Time to get back in the shade. "I don't know though. I love the games. It's all the travel I'm not used to. Maybe the second season would be easier because I'd be prepared."

"Like you said, we'll evaluate later." Mama linked arms with Kat, their heels tapping against the sidewalk. "Just remember you're coming home in a few weeks."

"The season won't end until the first week of September, but I'll be home after that."

There certainly wasn't anything to hold her in Cherry Hill. Even as the thought formed, she knew it wasn't true.

When they reached the hotel, Daddy led her to the car. A few minutes later they pulled up in front of her family's hotel. Mama looked back at her, a bright smile on her face. "In addition to everyone else, Mark's girl, Evelyn, is with us. I think you'll like her, Kat."

"Are they serious?"

"She's a WAVE, and they work together. She's an engineer, like Mark, on that top-secret project Mark can never talk about."

"Your mama's had the pleasure of leading her to the Lord."

"A real honor."

"What happened to Paige?" Kat couldn't imagine Mark with anyone who wasn't the perfect picture of femininity like Paige. That woman could grace any fashion magazine's pages. And to think she'd chosen to spend time with Mark. That still befuddled Kat.

Mama shrugged but didn't look disappointed. "They've gone their separate ways."

Kat had anticipated a different reaction if Mark and Paige ever moved on. Before she could probe deeper, Cassandra launched from the hotel.

"Katherine, you're finally here!" Kat barely had time to exit the car before Cassandra jumped into her arms. "I've waited ever so long to see you. Why'd you have to leave? Right when we moved home with you?" A pretty pout puckered Cassandra's lips.

"Cassandra, leave poor Kat alone." Josie trailed out of the room, Art Jr. balanced on her hip. "Hey, kiddo."

Kat rolled her eyes then set Cassandra down. "Hi, Josie. How's the little man?" She chucked Art under the chin. "He's grown a foot while I've been gone."

"Almost."

Mark joined the group, a pretty woman trailing him. Kat tried to focus on Mark, but she couldn't help her interest in this woman. And Mother and Daddy didn't mind. In fact they seemed excited. That wasn't typical for them. At all.

"Kat, I want you to meet Evelyn Happ. Evelyn, this is my kid sister." He wouldn't. Kat stepped back but not quickly enough to avoid a hair ruffling.

"I'm not a six-year-old child, Mark."

"You'll always be my kid sister."

"Maybe I should stay with the team after this. At least they treat me like an adult." She crossed her arms, trying not to be annoyed but failing. She'd forgotten what it felt like to be perpetually seen as the baby of the family. For heaven's sake, she was seventeen and had lived on her own all summer.

Evelyn winked at her. "You should hear how Mark brags about you. It's fair to say he's very proud of his kid sister."

Maybe she liked Evelyn after all.

Three hours later, Kat exhaled when her father dropped her off at the ballpark. All this family togetherness might kill her. Evelyn acted so perfect, with manners and speech that were flawless. No wonder her mother loved her. Even Josie had embraced her. And watching the look in Mark's eyes when his gaze followed her around the room left an empty feeling in the pit of Kat's stomach.

Love was in the air, and that meant change. Once he had a wife, Mark wouldn't have time for her. She felt petty even admitting that to herself.

He shouldn't need her. She was the baby in the family after all. But it felt different. Knowing he wouldn't follow her every game. Encourage her in baseball.

And even in her WAVE uniform, Evelyn exuded glamour.

Kat studied her image in the bathroom mirror. What man would ever be attracted to her?

She was a tomboy, with freckles dotting her nose and cheeks. Her short curls often looked matted from having a baseball cap clamped on top of them. Even when that hadn't happened, they rioted around her face in an out-of-control manner.

Nobody would ever want her. Jack's attention would disappear when he no longer needed her for his stories.

❧

A family filled one corner of the stands. The girl yelled encouragement to the Blossoms in a British accent. "Wallop the ball, Kat."

Jack watched them a moment. One of the women looked familiar. She must have been present when he had that conversation about Kat years ago at that game. She'd been a regular mama bear.

Kat shielded her eyes and searched the stands. When she found the group, she waved, a big enthusiastic sweep of her arm. She smiled, but a cord of tension stretched across her shoulders. Something bothered the young player, something very few would notice. Jack settled back, content to know he understood her. His gaze found her lips, and the memory of their kiss warmed him. Then he thought of that kid she'd left with instead of him.

Ed dropped onto the seat next to Jack, eyes dancing as he enjoyed his first road game with the Blossoms. "Our all-star brought some fans along."

"Yep, probably her family."

Ed rubbed his hands together. "Great! You can get some quotes from the proud parents for an article. Looks like her streak will continue. That girl's been a regular pay dirt of stories and quotes for you. The picture of innocence who plays like nobody's business."

A prickle poked Jack's conscience. Maybe Ed had nailed it. He used Kat, plain and simple. He'd never bothered to ask if she wanted to become a star. Instead he'd assumed she would. After all, who wouldn't? He'd decided she was the perfect candidate for it. She went along, while Faye and others worked for attention with a much more proactive approach to their publicity and articles. Jack dug into his box of Cracker Jack, ready to get his mind off that track.

"The readers love her." The words didn't make him feel better.

"True. Or maybe they like the image you've painted for them. All-American girl come to play ball. Fulfill a lifelong dream." Ed swigged his Coke. "I wonder if she has other dreams." He shrugged. "Doesn't really matter as long as readers keep buying the paper. You've done a great job with her, Jack."

Then why didn't it feel that way? What did he really know about Kat?

And what did he really want from a kid who was leaving in a few weeks?

The more the question rattled around his brain, the more he realized he didn't know her at all. He'd focused on the external, the easy-to-see parts of her. Though those were plenty fine, they didn't begin to delve into the woman lurking beneath the surface. The woman he'd kissed so thoroughly the other night.

"Go, Kat!" Jack shielded his eyes as he searched the stands for the source of the boisterous shout. There, a petite girl of about ten, sitting next to Kat's family. What were they like? Must be pretty amazing to have raised a girl like Kat. Maybe someday he'd know.

"That's it. Keep 'em coming, Kat." A man—her brother?—pumped his fist.

Ed chuckled. "You missed the play of the game. Good thing I'm here to fill you in on Kat and Lola's double play. The two combined for two outs, my boy." Ed swiped at a bead of sweat sitting on his bulbous nose. "Stars. All of 'em are stars."

The game ended with a win. Ed left with a jig in his step, and Jack headed to the field. He slowed his steps so he'd exit right after Kat's family. No need to rush, and maybe he'd learn something.

"Kat, you darted everywhere. I don't know how you do it, girl, but I'm proud of you." The man bear-hugged Kat, and she beamed, pure joy sparking in her eyes.

"Thanks, Daddy."

"Just remember you're coming home after the season."

Kat rolled her eyes. "I've promised, Dad. You know that. I'll come back, finish school, and then we'll see."

The man tweaked her nose. "I know. Call me foolish, but I need assurance this hasn't swept you away from us."

Her brother sidled up to her. "Give her a break, Dad. She's a good kid." He slugged her shoulder—quite the physical family. "Way to play. You must have learned from a pro."

"You know it, Mark." Kat wrinkled her nose at him. "See what I have to put up with, Evelyn? I do something well, and he wants the credit."

"Fishing for a compliment?" The gorgeous woman hanging on Mark's arm needled him.

Jack cleared his throat. "Good game, Katherine."

Kat jumped and spun in his direction. "Jack." A breathless quality accented the word. "I'd like you to meet my family. This is the man who decided it would be a good idea for all the players to trade kisses for war bonds. I helped him see the error of his ways."

"Be fair, Kat. Everyone thought it was a good idea."

"Which is why it got dropped from the festival." Kat rolled her eyes then grinned at her daddy. "See, you taught me well."

In a moment she'd introduced him to everyone, and Jack prayed there wouldn't be a quiz. Too many names, from too large a group.

"Would you like to join us for dinner, Mr. Raymond?" Kat's mother smiled, but a definite question lay in her eyes, the kind that made him wonder what would be grilled at dinner: the steak or him?

fifteen

"Jack, my boy, I've got the ticket for you." Ed rolled out of his office in his chair, pleased with himself over something.

Jack didn't really care what it was as long as it got his mind off the memory of watching Kat leave her house with that kid. Since returning to Cherry Hill, he'd worried there'd be a repeat event. The image remained locked in his mind. He needed to face the music. He had it bad for Kat.

If her kiss were any indication, she felt the same way he did but refused to acknowledge it. Her actions sure hadn't shown him she cared.

"Are you with me?"

Jack looked up from his typewriter, the one he hadn't typed a word on all day. "Sure."

"Tomorrow night you'll emcee the war-bond event. Your star ballplayers will sign autographs and do other things to encourage the fine folks of Cherry Hill to give their hard-earned dollars to the war effort."

"That doesn't sound too bad."

"It's not. Should be a piece of cake for a refined man like yourself." Ed shook his head, as if disgusted with Jack. "This is your chance to do something for the war. At least pretend a little enthusiasm."

"Yes sir!" Jack saluted Ed, who batted his hands at Jack and walked away.

"Always the kidder, aren't you?" Ed muttered as he headed to his office. "Maybe I should have kept this job for myself. You try to give a guy a break, a plum assignment, and he acts like he's too good for it."

Ed's door closed, blocking his words. Jack rolled his chair

away from his desk, leaned back, and locked his hands behind his head.

"You'd better get your tux out, Jack." Meredith leaned on his desk, one shapely leg crossed over the other.

"Yeah?"

"I've heard we'll have a movie star or two in town. Part of their war-bond efforts."

Jack sat up. That might make things more interesting.

"Thought that would get your attention." Meredith studied him until he had to fight the urge to squirm. "I don't know why you always have to play the hard guy. Ed's done nothing but give you breaks. So this isn't Chicago. What's the big deal? At least you've got a good job doing what you're good at. And you're safe while you do it. The least you can do is show some appreciation and a little enthusiasm on occasion."

"So you don't want my job after all. I'm touched."

Meredith stared at him then launched from his desk. "You are a piece of work."

Jack laughed as she stormed to her desk, grabbed her hat and purse, and headed to the door. "I need some fresh air."

With the room emptied, Jack leaned back again. Maybe he was the one who needed fresh air. Or a fresh perspective.

Ever since he'd accosted Kat—that word still made him cringe, but it best fit the situation—he'd felt bothered. Nothing could distract him from the fact that he hadn't shown himself to be a man worthy of her affection. Let alone worthy to hope that someday she could love him.

He treated everyone around him as if he were a porcupine, and none of them deserved that.

"Doreen, I'm headed to lunch."

"It's ten o'clock." She wrinkled her nose at him. "Didn't you have breakfast?"

"I'm hungry now." Jack bit back a growl. He didn't need an inquisition, just space.

"Okay." Doreen eyed him, as if checking for claws. "You

might try the farmers' market."

"Thanks." He strode from the building and stopped as the sun blinded him on the sidewalk.

What was that story? The one he'd learned in Sunday school? Some guy traveling on a highway only to be blinded by a bright light and hearing Jesus speak to him?

Jack turned right and wandered down Main Street. That encounter had changed the man's life. Hadn't the man persecuted believers and then become a chief proponent of the gospel? Jack didn't know why it had entered his mind, but the story remained firmly embedded in his thoughts. He reached a church, hesitated, and then walked in. Coolness embraced him when he stepped inside its shadows.

Paul? Was that the man's name?

A Bible sat on the back pew, and he picked it up. The leather cover felt rough but settled in his palm like it belonged there. He made his living with the written word but couldn't remember the last time he'd picked up a Bible. Must have been years earlier, before college.

"Can I help you, young man?"

Jack looked up to find a man standing in front of him, clad in jeans and a short-sleeved, button-down shirt. "Do I need to leave?"

"Oh no." Wire-rimmed glasses perched on the man's nose couldn't hide the curiosity and openness in his face. "I make it a practice to see if there's anything I can do to help those who find their way inside these doors."

"You don't need to worry about me. I'm fine." The man hesitated a moment, his smile never faltering. The longer he waited, the more Jack felt the compulsion to ask him a question. "Isn't there a story in here about a man blinded on a road? Maybe Paul?"

"You're on the right track. Paul was headed down one path, and God blinded him in order to get his attention. It worked. Paul left his dramatic encounter with God changed and then revolutionized the world for Christ." The man gestured to the space next to Jack. "May I?"

"Sure."

He settled onto the seat, hands loose in front of him as if he had all the time in the world to sit and contemplate with Jack. "What brings Paul to mind today?"

"Honestly? I'm not sure. It's been a long time since I've spent much time in church."

"Church is important." The man laughed. "But you could say I'm biased. I pastor this body, and I'm sure they'd be shocked to hear me say this, but church isn't the most important thing. The thing that matters for eternity is the state of your relationship with Jesus Christ. If He is the Son of God and Savior of your soul, then you've taken the first step. But He wants more. He wants to be the Lord of your life, the one you follow in all you do. If the church can help you learn how to do that, how to live for Him, then we've done our job.

"But if all you do is come to church because you think it's what you're supposed to do, then you could end up like your friend Paul. A man with tons of head knowledge but no real relationship with the Lord. And in trying to do what his knowledge told him was right, Paul worked in direct opposition to God. Not a position I ever want to find myself in."

Jack chewed on that a minute. "I'm still not sure why this came to mind now."

"Maybe it's God's way of getting your attention." The man considered Jack. "I've always been encouraged by the fact that Paul did horrific things to God's people, yet God still used Him mightily."

"Yes." Jack leaned back and considered the stained glass rising above the pulpit. The image of an empty tomb, with the stone rolled away, glowed in multihued color. He felt the tug of truth. That he had slipped away from something important and foundational to life. Jack ran his fingers over the Bible's surface. "Thank you for your time. You've given me something to chew on."

"Then I've done my job." The man slapped his hands on his thighs and pushed to his feet. "My name's Don Harrison. Feel free to take that Bible you're holding. We've got plenty more. And come by anytime to sit and contemplate or look for me, and we can chat more. The doors are open most of the time."

The man slipped up the aisle and then through a door off to the side of the pulpit. Jack sat a moment more before standing, the Bible held firmly in his grasp.

❧

The next evening Jack stood in front of his mirror, twisting his tuxedo bow tie back and forth. It didn't look right, but he couldn't figure out how to fix it. The clock on his table donged. Six o'clock. "Rats. I can't waste any more time on this."

He grabbed his hat but hesitated to put it on. No sense messing up his oiled hair.

Jack hurried outside, and the heaviness in the air felt like a wave of hot water had hit him. Blasted humidity. He'd be a sweaty mess before he reached the dance hall.

What had gotten into him?

He'd read the Bible the night before, reconnecting with the faith instilled in him as a child. Then today everything felt off. The time had come to make a decision, and that reality made him a bear.

Turning down the street, Jack mumbled to himself. He knew he had to get a grip before he reached the event. The charm would need to ooze from him in a thick, realistic way if people were going to buy war bonds. And that meant removing the weighty stone on his back that put him all out of sorts.

Fine. Jack stopped and planted his feet. Time to do what he knew was right.

All right, God. I know what You want. And I know it's the

right thing. I want You in control of my life, but I admit I'll fight You for it on occasion. No need to restart our relationship with lies. But teach me how to submit and live a life that honors You. Turn me into a Paul who can transform the world for You. Even here in Cherry Hill.

He waited but didn't feel the earth shift. "What did you expect?"

A lady weeding her victory garden looked at him with a half-fearful expression.

"Good evening, ma'am."

She nodded then watched as he walked past.

❧

Addebary had forced Kat to play a leading role tonight. No matter how she protested that anybody else would do a better job emceeing the war-bond dinner, he'd insisted the role was hers.

He certainly hadn't understood how much she hated public speaking. Playing in front of a crowd was one thing. She could hide inside her uniform. Speaking was completely different.

The butterflies stampeding through her stomach highlighted that fact.

Kat ran her hand down the emerald chiffon, floor-length gown she'd purchased for the event. She hoped she didn't look a fool, but she'd had to buy a dress to play the part. It wasn't like she'd brought an evening gown to Cherry Hill. Times like this, she wished Mama or Josie lived closer. But a couple of the other players had gone with her and had at least given her feedback. Though when Rosie had held up the black gown, Kat had put her foot down.

It was a fund-raiser not a funeral.

Kat glanced in the mirror and practiced her smile. Her lips twitched at the edges, but no one would notice that from a distance. If she were lucky, her mystery fellow emcee wouldn't notice either. And her nerves would remain her secret.

Mrs. Harrison knocked on her door. "You look lovely, Kat."

"Thank you." She looked in the mirror one last time, practiced her smile, then turned. "Am I missing anything?"

"Just this." Her landlady stepped in with a strand of pearls in her hand. "These will be the perfect touch."

"I can't wear those."

"Yes, you can. My little contribution to the effort. I don't wear them often now that I have children to yank on them." She chattered while she affixed the strand behind Kat's neck. "Let's see. Your hair. We need to sweep it up. Then you'll have the perfect look."

A few minutes later Kat looked in the mirror and had to admit Mrs. Harrison had been right. The pearls and upsweep transformed her into a woman she hardly recognized. She suddenly felt like Cinderella headed to the ball. Maybe she'd find her Prince Charming. Her cheeks warmed at the ridiculous thought. "Thank you."

"You're welcome. Have a great time, and tell me all about it in the morning." Mrs. Harrison's smile didn't quite hide the shadow in her eyes. "Mr. Harrison's ready to give you a ride. And don't forget to get a taxi to bring you home. You can't traipse through Cherry Hill in that gown and those shoes."

Kat smiled at the mothering. She might not have Mama here, but God had surrounded her with a family who cared.

Mr. Harrison opened the door for her with a bow. And the night only grew more magical as she stepped from the car and entered the country club. Someone had spent hours decorating and had transformed the entryway with strung lights and more tulle than she'd seen since Josie's wedding.

She waltzed up the stairs and through the doors.

The buzz of at least a hundred murmuring voices filled the hall. She didn't want to think about how many people attended. Instead she focused on the rainbow of gowns. Hers fit right in with the elegant yet simple note most of the women had hit.

"There you are." Ed Plunkett, the editor of the paper, slid next to her. "Our own Cherry Hill Blossoms star."

Kat felt heat climb her neck at his words. "I'm not really a star."

"Tonight you are." He took her arm and guided her through the hall. "We've got a couple B-list stars here including Victoria Hyde and Robert Garfield. But don't worry, you'll outshine them all."

"Do you really need me?" *Please say no.*

"Of course. Local talent and all that." He slowed and scanned the crowd before taking off again. "Ah, here we go. Your fellow emcee."

A man turned and looked at her, his gaze taking in every inch of her, a slow smile growing on his face.

sixteen

Katherine Miller took his breath away. From the red curls piled on top of her head to the tips of her black shoes peeking out from the hem of her green dress, the girl had metamorphosed into a woman.

The shortstop had disappeared, hidden in a gown designed for a princess.

Jack bowed and offered his arm. "Mademoiselle."

A pinch of color appeared on each cheek. "Jack."

The way his name slipped off her tongue, he wanted her to say it again.

"All right, you two. You have a job to do tonight. Once that's done, you can stare at each other all you want."

Color rushed up her neck in a manner that made Jack want to slug Ed. All he could do was deflect the attention from her. "I'll get Miss Miller up to speed." She shot a look at him—probably from the use of her formal name. But he had to do something to create a distance between them. Otherwise his emcee duties would fall to the side as he swept her into his arms and danced the night away.

"I wouldn't mind the overview." Her voice had an edge to it. So she didn't appreciate his efforts. He'd make a note of that.

Ed ran them through the lineup then left to find his movie stars.

No way Victoria Hyde could look as good as his Kat.

Whoa.

His Kat. He needed to rein that thought in. . .fast.

Before Jack could do or say anything to reveal his thoughts, the mayor stepped up to be introduced to Kat. In mere minutes men surrounded her, and Jack found himself on the outside of the circle. It was as if all the men recognized that Kat was a beautiful flower ready to be picked. The thought unsettled him. He didn't know which was worse: watching her like some grouchy sentinel or recognizing that he might have competition from real men for her attention and affection. That kid didn't stand a chance now. . .but Jack himself might not either.

And how did all this fit in with his new commitment to a life of faith?

His head hurt just thinking the questions.

She looked over the crowd until their gazes connected. He read her silent plea and slipped through the assembled men.

"I think you promised me this dance." The thought of her in his arms made him giddy.

A soft smile tipped her lips. "If you'll excuse me, gentlemen."

The men grumbled but parted, allowing the two to pass.

Kat's shoulders relaxed. "Could we get a glass of punch instead?"

Jack changed directions and led her to the punch and hors d'oeuvres. "Are you ready for tonight?"

She shook her head. "I hate speaking." She put her hand over her mouth, as if to stop more words from escaping.

"A fear?"

She nodded.

"I'm not so fond of it myself." Jack shrugged and tucked his hands deep in his pockets. "Guess it's a part of life."

"Yeah. Thanks for making me a star." Sarcasm laced her sentence.

"Here to serve."

The band ended the song, and the bandleader invited attendees to take their seats. "I think that's our cue."

She glided through the crowd to the head table. As he watched her, Jack forgot about the age difference. All he saw was a woman, one who had captured his interest and his heart.

❧

Kat's heart beat wildly in her throat. A waiter swooped her salad plate away, replacing it with the main course. Jack sat next to her, playing the perfect gentleman. It seemed like a switch had turned in him when he saw her on Ed's arm. As if tonight he saw her as more than a ball-playing high school student. The ember that occasionally appeared in his gaze had flared to life. The thought both excited and terrified her.

What had she experienced of life? Not enough to cause a man like Jack to love her.

And to tell him her fear without a thought? She'd lost her mind.

And her heart.

That thought made her drop her fork, and it clattered to the floor. So much for appearing the sophisticated woman. What a fraud.

Victoria Hyde sat to the left of Jack and smiled at her. "Don't worry. It happens to the best of us."

Robert Garfield nodded. "All the time. Don't let it bother you."

The evening could only get better. After all, she'd only embarrassed herself in front of movie stars and the man she loved. She longed to sink through the floor.

The band struck a few quick notes, the cue to begin the program, and she launched to her feet. The chair tipped behind her and would have fallen if Jack hadn't caught and righted it. "You okay?"

She nodded fiercely, sure she looked even more like an idiot. "Can we get this over with?"

"Only if you take a deep breath and look at me."

"No." She didn't need him to see the terror that burned through her like a white-hot fire. Couldn't risk him seeing her fight the nausea that threatened to reject her salad. That humiliation would topple her after everything else.

Jack grabbed her hand, caressed her fingers, the sensation

pulling her thoughts from her stomach. "You can do this, Kat."

"Because I'm your handcrafted puppet?"

"No, because you're an amazing young woman. You have the poise and ability to do this with grace and style. Now get up there, and show everyone what I already know. That you are a fascinating person they'll be blessed to meet."

If he kept talking like that, she'd walk to the moon. "Yes, Jack."

She followed him to the podium, suddenly feeling like Katharine Hepburn when she followed Cary Grant's character in *Bringing Up Baby*. She needed to be more than his shadow, even if he was the reason she could find the strength to stand there. People had come to buy war bonds and support the war effort, so she needed to do her part and get them excited. If only she knew how.

❧

Kat transformed in front of Jack. Her chin came up, her fingers stopped twitching with the fabric of her gown, and a real sparkle bubbled in her eyes. It was like watching Snow White come to life when the prince kissed her. Jack took a step back and let her precede him to the podium.

"Good evening, Jack." Her gaze embraced him before she turned to the audience.

"Kat." He looked at the crowd, a blur in the haze behind the spotlight that engulfed them. "And good evening to all you fine folks out there." A roar erupted from the crowd. "Tonight we're here to raise money for the war effort."

Kat leaned in, and he paused. "With a little help from two movie stars come all the way from Hollywood to spend the night with us." The crowd tittered, and flames erupted in her cheeks as she must have realized what she'd said. "I mean—"

"Please welcome Victoria Hyde and Robert Garfield." Jack gestured toward each star, and the crowd welcomed them with all the warmth he expected from Cherry Hill's residents. He even heard a few wolf whistles mixed in with the applause.

The stars stood, waved, and then bowed and curtsied. "They'll join us up here in a few minutes." Jack looked at the cards Ed had left on the podium for them. They might not need the prompts at the rate they were going. "Katherine Miller, you look splendid tonight. Let everyone see how lovely you look."

Kat stepped out from behind the podium and posed for the crowd. "Why thank you, Jack. It is a bit different from my usual uniform."

"Mm-hm." The crowd laughed with him. "So what brings you here?"

"Other than getting to play dress-up for an evening?" She batted her eyelashes at him. She had no idea how fetching and magical she looked. "Here to do my part for the boys." She looked him up and down for a moment, and he wondered what was running through her mind. "Jack, you wear that tux like it was made for you. Not quite what the boys in uniform wear."

The crowd laughed with her, but Jack froze. Her eyes remained guileless. His head knew she hadn't meant anything by the remark, but as laughter rolled across the auditorium, he didn't care. He felt the reality of it.

Everyone here would think he'd shirked his duty to fight. Just another pretty boy. And none of them would ever care to know the truth: that the military wouldn't have him.

❧

A wall slammed into place between Jack and Kat, but she didn't know why. As the crowd laughed, she searched her mind for a reason. The laughter died down, but Jack remained silent. Kat hurried through the next particulars then invited the stars to the podium. Their job was to launch the bond sale with a flurry of support.

While the stars worked their magic, Jack and Kat returned to their seats. He acted the perfect gentleman, but he'd disappeared. He sat next to her, back ramrod stiff.

"Jack, what is it?"

He chewed on his lower lip but didn't turn in her direction.

"Please, if I said or did something, you need to tell me. I can't apologize for what I don't understand."

"It's nothing, Kat. Really."

The words were right, but she didn't believe him. Should she push to get an answer from him? Was this the place? As he fiddled with his cuff links, she knew she had to try. "I'm sorry."

He sighed, still not looking at her. "I know."

"Are you going to tell me what I'm sorry about?"

"Do you really think I'm hiding rather than fighting?"

"No." Her fingers played with her purse strap where it lay in her lap. Suddenly it hit her. "Jack, I'm so sorry that you think I meant that with my comment. See this is why I hate speaking. Things always come out wrong."

"Not quite what the boys are wearing." His tone mocked hers.

"I'm sorry."

He took a deep breath then blew it out until there couldn't be any air left in his lungs. "I know."

"So get up there, and make fun of me next. You can even be intentional about it."

"No, thank you. No one would believe me. And I'd be a terrible emcee."

"Well, aren't you?" She giggled as he shot her a look that should have made her squirm. "Look, you're stuck with me for the night. Let's make the best of it. Then I'll write a formal apology that your paper can print."

He grimaced.

"Fine, you come up with the mea culpa since all my ideas give you indigestion."

The embers reignited in his eyes.

"On second thought, I revoke that offer. Just forgive me."

"Already have. But I think it's too late to revoke your offer, little girl. I like the idea of writing the retraction."

As he said the words, for once she didn't protest. Instead she let them settle over her like a term of endearment.

"We have unfinished business." He grinned at her like he wanted to sweep her out of the chair and into his embrace. "But that can wait. Until I take you home tonight."

The way he said the words made her stomach jump with anticipation touched with fear.

Kat tried to focus on her hostess duties as the night wore on. The citizens bought war bonds like it was a contest to see who could give more. The stars autographed photos as part of the incentive to buy. Kat slid to the background and allowed Jack to cajole the crowd to give more and more. Almost as if the more he talked, the more they'd forget her offhand comment.

Finally the night ended, and Ed released them to go home. Addebary walked up to her as she hit the door.

"Good job, kid. I knew you had it in you. See you in a few hours for practice." He ambled off, a baseball cap slammed on his head—a definite oddity in the crowd.

"I think I have you to myself now." Jack swung her around then pulled her tight to his side. He groaned when a group of local businessmen stopped them for congratulatory remarks. "Thanks, gents. Time to get the star home before practice." He led her to a waiting taxi. After settling her into the cab and sliding in next to her, he rattled off her address.

An awkward silence settled over the cab. After a few minutes the taxi pulled in front of the Harrisons' house, and Kat opened her mouth to thank Jack for the ride. He placed a finger against her lips, stilling her words.

He studied her face, seeming to memorize every feature. She fought the urge to look away. She wasn't a child and needed to act the part of an adult.

"You kids getting out, or do I keep my meter running?"

Kat jerked back and laughed as Jack pulled out money for the fare. "Thanks, Gramps."

"Just helping young love along."

Jack helped Kat from the cab and walked her to the door. "I don't think we need any help."

She stood, back against the door, mesmerized by him. Her breath hitched, and then he leaned forward. His lips brushed hers, and an electric shock charged the air. "Good night, princess."

He walked down the sidewalk whistling an off-key tune, while Kat tried to catch her breath.

seventeen

Jack grabbed a copy of the paper as he strode through the door. A photo of Kat and him in full emcee role blazed across the top of the front page, the crowd laughing and Kat grinning in that irrepressible way of hers.

Princess. That's what he'd called her, but last night he meant something completely new. It wasn't the fact she'd been dressed up and looked like a princess. No, something deeper had settled inside him as he watched her fight her fear.

"Here comes the conquering hero." Ed grinned as he swaggered from his office. "I told you, you'd be great."

"I guess you did."

"Record numbers raised last night. Good work."

"I don't know that we had anything to do with it."

"Maybe not, but I wouldn't bet against you." Ed rubbed his hands together. "We may have to bring that kid back for other events. The two of you were total magic. Fire and ice."

Jack didn't need to ask who filled which role. No, he hadn't warmed up until the night ended. Then it had taken an ironclad act of will to walk away from Kat with the warmth of her kiss scorching through him.

"Well, back to the Cherry Hill Festival." Ed shook his head. "You sure know how to kick one off." Ed headed to his office then stopped just inside the door. "Come see me, once you're settled. I've got something to run by you. Something I think you'll like."

Jack tossed his hat on his desk and grabbed a pencil. He didn't like the way his thoughts cycled back to Kat at any unguarded moment. If she ever figured out the trend, he'd be exposed. Vulnerable.

Could he handle that?

Could he entrust his heart to her?

Did he want to?

The pencil broke in Jack's grip. Whatever Ed had for him had to be better than this.

Jack strode into the office and plopped into the battered chair in front of Ed's desk. Ed had his back turned to him, phone pressed to his ear. "Yeah, he just barged in. I think he'll be excited to consider your offer." Jack leaned forward at the words. What kind of offer would involve him? "We'll be in touch."

Ed hung up then ran his fingers through what was left of his hair, ending with a shaking motion at the base of his scalp. "Still eager to leave Cherry Hill?"

Jack considered his words carefully. "Maybe."

"Thought that might be your answer, seeing how a little woman is here."

"That can't go anywhere."

"Really?" Ed watched him like Jack had turned into prey he couldn't wait to devour. "I expected you to stonewall, but I'm no fool. There's something special between the two of you when you aren't denying it."

Jack started to protest, but Ed stopped him. "Hear me out."

"All right." Jack settled back and crossed his arms.

"Would you be more or less interested in this certain someone if you weren't bound to be separated in a few weeks?"

"More, but what's the point? There's no way her parents will let her stay here. Cherry Hill isn't as important as finishing high school." And he couldn't blame them. That's why he couldn't do anything to make his feelings official. He rubbed his neck. Though he'd let his emotions leap ahead last night.

Ed rubbed his hands together like a boy ready to get the gift of his life. "What if I had the solution for you?"

"When did you metamorphose into a matchmaker?"

"I'm a romantic at heart."

Jack snorted then coughed to cover it. "I'm listening."

"Good." Ed pulled a paper from beneath a stack on his desk. He tossed it at Jack, who read the masthead.

"*Dayton Times*?"

"Yep. A buddy of mine from college is now managing the city desk for the paper. He's short staffed. thanks to the war. Asked if I knew anyone who could tackle the city beat without a lot of training. You came to mind." Ed grinned like he'd handed Jack the Holy Grail of journalism.

"It isn't exactly Chicago."

"Nuts." Ed batted his hands at Jack. "Why this crazy fixation with Chicago? Move to Dayton, do a good job, and you'll find yourself a step closer to that city."

Jack considered the idea. "What's the salary?"

"You'll have to ask Pete. If you like the idea, he wants you in two weeks."

That fast? "It's been years since I spent one day in Dayton."

"What's to know? It's a small city. In the Midwest."

As if that explained everything. "I'll think about it."

"Do that. And when you're ready, here's Pete's number."

Jack took the piece of paper, tucked it in his pocket. "Are you that eager to get rid of me?"

Ed shook his head. "Just a—"

"I know. . .a romantic."

He left the office, mind spinning. Maybe this was something he should pray about. What if Kat didn't want him to follow her? Had he imagined her response to his kiss last night? Doubts assailed him.

The next day Jack walked up the steps of the Cherry Hill Community Church. He couldn't think of a time he'd attended church for anything other than a wedding or funeral. While he nodded at people he knew, a certain redhead sat halfway up the sanctuary by herself. He eased onto the pew next to her.

"Mind if I join you?"

She shook her head, the ghost of a smile turning up her lips.

Chords of music poured from the organ, and he turned his attention to the front. The peace of worshipping crested over him.

To think he'd turned away from this. He'd been a fool to pretend he didn't need God. As the hymn ended and the pastor walked to the podium, Jack leaned forward. What wisdom would this man impart during the sermon?

❧

Another road trip then a quick series at home. The pace wouldn't ease before the playoffs. In the moments she had to herself, Kat couldn't believe her time with the Blossoms would end in mere weeks.

Jack showed up at the clubhouse, did the routine interviews, but through all of them seemed distracted. He might have sat next to her at church, but he hadn't said much to her afterward. And now he read a Bible on the train, too. Kat almost didn't know what to make of the change. Still, he seemed distant. He hardly looked at her, while her lips tingled each time she saw him.

She didn't know whether to shake him or hit him.

But any time she tried to get him alone to ask what was going on, he disappeared like he'd turned into a vapor.

One day she must not have covered her consternation when she watched him from across the diamond. Faye sidled next to her, hand and glove on her hips. "Get your head in the game, Kat."

"Sorry." Kat fluffed the curls that perspiration had adhered to her neck.

"We need you focused if we're going to win and move up in the standings." Faye glanced at Jack where he hunched on a bench. "Don't worry. He'll come around."

Kat tried to push the thought from her mind before it led to the next. Did she want him around? The answer was a resounding yes. But what if he didn't want her? Argh, she couldn't do this. Not now.

She forced her attention back to the game, what they paid her to do. Catch that little ball and prevent scores. She might not be able to interpret Jack's silence or force him back to her, but she could control her efforts. The rest she had to leave to God. Silence her fears and trust Him to know what was best for her future.

The crack of a bat connecting with a ball brought her attention sharply to focus. She sidestepped toward the ball, reaching it just as Rosie did. They collided, but Rosie came up with the ball. She waved it at the crowd while Kat stood and dusted off her uniform. Rosie grinned then tossed the ball to the pitcher. She turned her back to the stands, huffing. "Don't make me run like that again."

Kat bit her tongue. It wasn't her fault Rosie hadn't stayed in her area.

"Next time you're daydreaming I may not reach the ball in time."

"I'll keep that in mind."

Addebary signaled the umpire and trotted out to where they stood. "Is there a problem, ladies?"

"No sir." Kat shook her head.

"Then let's play the game if you don't mind. That's what our fans paid to see."

Rosie walked away with a flounce of her skirt. A man in the second row whistled, and Kat blushed for Rosie.

"Come on, Miller. Get in the game."

"Yes sir." Kat squared her shoulders. Thoughts of Jack and the confusion he generated in her had to wait.

After the Blossoms squeaked out a win, Jack disappeared again. Somehow he managed to write articles that included highlights of what she did during the game. But if he did it again, he would do it without talking to her since all she saw was his back as he left.

Fine! If that's how he wanted to be, she'd cooperate. No more wasted thoughts on him, especially when they interfered with her playing. No one had ever done that. Before Jack.

❧

Jack walked through his thinking one more time. He couldn't make this change without knowing he did it for the right reasons. Would he resent it if he moved and then Kat forgot about him? He had a feeling he'd make sure that didn't happen, but what if?

He'd prayed the best way he knew how. He'd read his Bible. He'd talked to the pastor.

Nothing seemed to stand in his way. Instead everything pointed toward the move.

Even his landlord was eager to have him break his lease so she could re-let the apartment at a higher rate. It almost felt too easy.

Was that a sign?

The pastor had told him to pray, read the Bible, and ask for peace. If he had peace and couldn't find reasons to stay, then he should step out in faith. Easy for a pastor to say. After all, he was paid to have faith.

Jack's recent steps of faith were new enough that he didn't know if he could trust them. Would he even know if God told him to stay?

The questions pained his mind. Stretched his understanding.

All he knew was he had to make a decision.

Jack marched into Ed's vacant office and picked up the phone. After a few attempts Doreen got him connected with the Dayton paper.

"Jack Raymond calling for Pete Hodges."

After several minutes a gruff voice answered. "Hodges."

"Sir, this is Jack Raymond."

"About time you called."

"Yes, sir."

"So, are you taking the position? Ready to work harder than you ever have?"

"You certainly know how to sell a man on the job."

Rough laughter carried over the line. "Blunt, aren't you? I like that in a reporter. You'll need that around here. This isn't Cherry Hill."

"That's what I'm counting on."

They talked details, and when he hung up, Jack wiped sweat from his forehead. He'd done it. He was Dayton bound. Now to tell Kat. He needed to think of the right way. A way that would make it a memory worthy of a promise he hoped would last forever.

❧

A rare day arrived that week. The Blossoms had a day without a game. Kat lounged in bed for an extra hour, while the sun lit patterns on the patchwork quilt, then got up to help Mrs. Harrison with her children. A series of clouds brought a brief rain shower, perfect for creating puddles for the three oldest children to splash in when she took them to the library late that morning. After corralling them home, a bit soaked but grinning, Kat wondered how Mrs. Harrison found the energy to umpire them every day. Mothering was exhausting work.

When Kat stepped into the kitchen, a fragrant sweetness tickled her nose.

"These came while you were out." Mrs. Harrison pointed her chin at a bouquet of flowers while she continued to chop carrots.

"For me?" A pounding filled Kat's ears at the thought someone had sent her flowers.

"Yes, but you'll have to read the card to see from who. I didn't open it."

"Thank you." Kat grabbed the card and rushed to her room. Flouncing on her bed, she opened the note. *Will you honor me by joining me for dinner? Jack. P.S. Joanie Devons gave her approval.*

The last words brought a smile. How thoughtful that he checked before asking.

She stood and called to accept before she could think too hard. After a few moments the operator connected her to the paper. "Is Jack there?"

"No, honey. Can I take a message?"

Kat hesitated. What could she leave in the message? Besides, the petty part of her wanted to punish him for his weeklong silence by saying no. But she had three weeks left in Cherry Hill. She didn't want to waste them apart from Jack. Not if the possibility of more lingered between them. "Yes, if you could tell him—"

"Oh, wait a minute. Here he comes." There was a muffled sound then scattered words. "Here he is."

"Jack Raymond." At the sound of his rich voice, Kat's mind blanked. "Hello?"

"Um, hi." Way to sound like a sophisticated woman. Kate Hepburn would have said something—anything!—better. "This is Katherine. Katherine Miller."

"Hey, princess."

With that word her pulse slowed, and her thoughts ordered. "Hi. Thanks for the flowers. They're beautiful."

"You're welcome." She didn't know why, but she'd expected more.

"So. Are you still free tonight?" If he hadn't thought she was a kid before, he certainly must now. Could she be any more tongue-tied?

Silence filled the air. She knew it. He regretted sending the invitation. She dropped her forehead to her hand and stifled a groan.

"Only if you can join me." She could sense his smile over the wire.

Her heart began to race. "I can."

"Good. I'll pick you up at seven."

Just like that they had an official date. A moment later Kat hung up and leaned against the counter.

"Good news?" Mrs. Harrison smiled as she watched Kat.

"The best. I think." She chewed on a fingernail. How should she dress for the mystery date?

Tonight might answer some of her questions. She needed to learn if they could ever have more than friendship before she moved home. That much she had to know.

The rest could wait.

eighteen

It had to be a rule somewhere that you didn't take a woman out to dinner in your shirtsleeves. Jack strolled up the Harrisons' sidewalk, the muggy weather making him wish he'd broken that rule and left his suit coat at home. He felt rings of sweat at his neck and underarms. Not the suave image he'd tried to achieve.

He certainly wasn't William Holden.

But he didn't want a Hollywood life filled with glamour and fame. He couldn't stand glitz and fakeness. What he wanted was a relatively simple life. Work hard. Play hard. Love hard.

And every time he pictured the love hard part, a certain redhead with springy curls and lots of freckles dotting her pert nose played the starring role. He couldn't imagine anyone else in that role. Frankly he didn't want to.

He hoped the flowers he held didn't tip the scales over the top. The fresh-faced daisies were different from the fancy bouquet the florist had fashioned earlier for Kat. Jack wanted Kat to know he saw the woman lurking beneath the surface. But he also knew the fresh-faced girl—she was the one who'd captured his imagination. His attention. His heart.

Hopping the last two steps, Jack rapped on the door. A few moments later Mr. Harrison came to the door. "Should I ask what your intentions are, young man?" His words were harsh but softened by a smile.

"That might be taking the pseudo dad role a bit far."

"Agreed." Mr. Harrison opened the door. "Come on in. I'm not sure, but I think she's doing something last-minute, like powdering her nose. I'm relieved my girl's not old enough yet for scoundrels like you."

"Yes, sir." They passed the minutes talking about the latest news from the front. The Italians were abandoning Sicily while the Solomon Islands were under attack. The men agreed they were ready for some good news. "Let's hope the Allies keep the Italians on the move."

The soft clomp of heels sinking into carpet finally reached his ears. Jack struggled off the davenport and onto his feet. Kat wore a soft blue dress with flared skirt that emphasized her tiny waist. He could get used to seeing her in real clothes rather than her uniform and practice clothes.

"Hello, Jack." A flash of something—expectation?—filled her doelike eyes.

"Katherine. These are for you." He held out the daisies and enjoyed the soft blush that colored her cheeks.

"They're beautiful. Thank you."

"Almost as pretty as you."

"Let me put them in some water." Katherine hurried from the room, returning a minute later.

"Are you ready to head out?" She nodded, and he turned to Mr. Harrison. "A pleasure talking with you, sir."

"You, too, Jack. It's not every night I get to talk with someone as up on the wires as a newspaperman. Now don't keep the girl out late. I'd hate to have to chase you down with my shotgun."

The soft color in Kat's cheeks deepened. Jack offered his arm and then ushered her outside. "Do you mind if we walk the few blocks downtown?"

"If I did, it'd be a bit late, wouldn't it?"

"Touché, mademoiselle."

"It's a good thing I like exercise." Kat did a shuffle step around him as if she'd transformed into Ginger Rogers. Too bad he wasn't Fred Astaire. "Thank you for the flowers. They're beautiful."

"Not as beautiful as you."

She stopped and looked at him, searching past his walls. "Is that a line?"

Jack matched her gaze. "No, Katherine Miller, it's not."

"Good." She turned so she was shoulder to shoulder with him, and he instantly missed the connection. "I'd hate to have to evaluate every word you say tonight."

Jack snorted. "You are something else."

"That's what my brother tells me."

They strolled downtown, the conversation light and easy. How did she manage to do that? She gave no indication she tried to impress. Instead Kat was who she was. Did she understand that's what made her so incredibly special and unique? They passed the Italian restaurant with its rich, spicy aroma then sidestepped a couple exiting a Chinese eatery. The ginger twanged his nose. Kat didn't seem interested in either. Instead she kept up a steady flow of stories about her family and home. They came to life as she mimicked voices and gestured with abandon. She swung an arm, and he ducked.

She stopped, giggling behind her hand. "Sorry about that."

"You are nothing if not enthusiastic about life."

"That's one way to describe it." She shrugged. "I talk with my hands when I get nervous. If people are ducking for their lives, then they aren't watching me."

Jack stopped and brushed a soft curl that had escaped her hat. "I like watching you."

"Why?" He almost missed the whispered word.

Here it was. That all-important moment to convince her he saw to the heart of her.

"I mean, there are so many women around here who would love your company. Why not Faye or Rosie? Or anyone else?" She took a breath then forged ahead. "Why me? I'm nothing but a kid compared to them."

"I don't want to compare you to anyone, Kat. God's made you into an amazing young woman with the promise of a lifetime of depth and character." That didn't sound quite right. He worked with words, for goodness' sake. Couldn't he get this right? "Doesn't 1 Timothy talk about not letting anyone look down on you because of your youth? So shouldn't you stop doing that? Sure you're younger than me. It's not the first time in history that's happened. Let's try this, see where it leads."

A cloud formed on her brow. That definitely hadn't come out right.

So Jack tipped her chin up and communicated in a way that words couldn't destroy.

❧

His lips settled on hers, and Kat momentarily forgot where she was. She longed to forget everything. To trust Jack's words at face value, but she had to guard her heart. In his kiss she sensed a commitment, but he hadn't said the words yet. Until he did, she had to put distance between them. Especially when chances were it would all end in a matter of weeks anyway.

Someone wolf whistled behind them. Kat startled and pushed against Jack's chest. The kiss intensified, then he stepped back.

Kat sucked in a breath. "You—we—we can't do that, Jack." She pressed a trembling hand into her stomach, trying to calm the riot of butterflies storming inside. A hooded look cloaked his eyes as he searched her face.

He nodded. "Of course, you're right."

"I'm missing something." She waggled her fingers in his face, emphasizing the ring finger. "I have to be careful until I'm wearing that special something."

Jack shook his head and laughed. "You are the most amazing woman, Katherine Miller."

As they continued down the sidewalk, she hoped he meant it. Because all she wanted was to be the woman he could never forget.

They circled downtown, and Kat wondered if Jack intended to take her somewhere for dinner. Her stomach rumbled, and he must have heard.

"Ready for some food?"

She nodded. Maybe she should lower her hopes from the candlelit dinners she read about in all those dime-store novels. Maybe reality didn't match the images she'd read.

Jack glanced at his watch. "We've got time for dinner before I take you to the movie. Let's eat here." He opened the door and ushered her into a diner. From the first glance it didn't look like much. Kat hoped she wouldn't find cockroaches in the corners if she looked closely. Maybe she'd better keep her eyes half shut.

"Are you sure it's okay?"

"Don't let the look dissuade you. They put all their effort into the cuisine."

"Cuisine. I hope it lives up to the label."

"It will, or I'll eat my hat."

"Anything has to taste better than that."

"Are you kidding?" Jack tapped the top of his hat. "This is premium straw, princess."

A waitress walked up. "Table for two?"

"Yes, and a quiet corner, please."

Kat closed her eyes as the waitress led them to a small table. *This would be good. This would be good. This would be good.* Jack wasn't trying to kill her. Kat opened her eyes and settled onto a bistro chair. The waitress handed them single-sheet menus and left after reciting the daily specials.

"Recommend anything?"

"Trust me, it's all good." Jack ran a finger down the menu. "Try the steak or pork chops."

Kat's stomach lurched then grumbled. "I guess it doesn't care what I eat as long as it's food."

They shared a laugh and chatted as the waitress took their orders and brought Cokes. By the time their entrées arrived, though, Jack had retreated. He still participated in the conversation, but something weighed on him. Should she ask or wait him out? This was so different from the group outings she'd had with other high schoolers back home. Maybe that was it. She'd done something to remind him she was too young for him. It was one thing to quote a Bible verse to her. Another thing completely to spend concentrated time with her.

Kat chewed a bite of the perfectly cooked steak, savoring the flavor and choosing her words. She swallowed and took the plunge. "Jack, I understand if you want to cut tonight short. Feel free to take me home after dinner."

"What? Is that what you want?" Confusion tightened his posture.

"No, but you're so quiet I thought I bored you. I mean, I understand if I do."

"No, Kat." He reached for her hand and stroked it with his thumb. "It's not that. I have something to tell you. Something I hope will make you as excited as I am."

"Are you headed overseas?"

"No." He drew the word out, turning it into multisyllables. "I didn't think you'd be eager for me to go that far away."

"Isn't that what you want?"

"A bigger paper would be nice, but I've found one a lot closer to home. A lot closer to you."

"To me?"

"I've accepted a job with the *Dayton Times*." His smile stretched from ear to ear, while her thoughts raced.

"You're moving to Dayton?" She felt like a parrot, echoing his words.

"Next week."

"Next week?" She shook her head, trying to dislodge the echo.

Jack nodded, a wary expression crossing his face. "Next week. I thought you'd be glad to hear this."

Her eyebrows drew together, and her mouth opened; she tried to relax her face. "I am. You surprised me. That's all."

Jack leaned toward her, elbows planted on the table, tie

dangerously close to landing in his mashed potatoes. "Kat, we can't test the future if I'm here and you're in Dayton. It's too far, and you have to finish school." He stated the words matter-of-factly, starkly. "There's something here." He gestured between them. "I sense it and know you do, too. I want to see where it leads."

"I do, too." Kat licked her lips and tried to swallow around a sudden mountain blocking her throat. "Moving. Jeepers. That's serious."

"Yes."

That single word hovered between them. Kat shifted, fingers of discomfort climbing her spine. Yes, she wanted a deeper relationship with Jack. More than friendship. But this? Now she squirmed at the thought of what he'd done for her. "You didn't have to."

Jack ran his fingers through his hair and leaned back. "I already did. I had hoped you'd like this."

Kat pushed a smile on her face, knowing it didn't hide the storm of confusion in her eyes. "I'm surprised. That's all." Jack started to push back from the table, but she grabbed his hand, silently begging him to stay. "Thank you."

"You're welcome." He slouched. "I don't want to pressure you for more than you're ready for, Kat. But you are the girl who waggled her fingers at me earlier. The only way that can happen is if we're in the same town and can try a relationship without the craziness of the baseball season. We need to see what we're like in normal life." He took a breath and considered her. "There's something special between us. You liven my life in a way no one else has. I don't want to lose that before we see what God has for us."

"I love how you've dived into your relationship with God."

"That's thanks to you. I want to be the man you can love."

"You already are."

Jack glowed at her words. "Then you aren't upset that I'm coming to Dayton?"

"No." She really wasn't. And as she looked at him, she knew she couldn't say anything else. And she really was excited, wasn't she, under the layers of shock and wariness?

nineteen

The jitters wouldn't leave Kat alone.

She'd always expected to feel ecstatic after reaching an understanding with a young man. Isn't that what happened to the heroines in most romances? Instead she felt trapped in a screwball comedy and couldn't figure out how to escape.

Jack was attentive but distracted. And then he moved, with promises they'd see each other often once she returned home.

Would that happen?

There'd be the added scrutiny of her father, a welcome occurrence, but few boys withstood it long. Would Jack be different?

And then there'd be their schedules. She doubted he'd eagerly escort her to homecoming. And would he proudly take her to his work affairs? It would be a far cry from him shadowing the team.

His move brought a wave of pressure she'd never anticipated.

Kat prayed about it. It was all she knew to do. Ultimately it remained the best thing she could do. Much better than continued fretting.

What if Jack was the one?

Wasn't it the perfect example of something only God could orchestrate? How else could a girl from Ohio meet a man living in Indiana and fall in love? The thought brought a peace she clung to. And if God wasn't in it, He'd let her know. If she somehow missed God's direction, she had no doubt Mama would get the message and clue her in. If anyone had a direct line to God, Mama did.

Someday Kat hoped she had a faith that mirrored Mama's. And just maybe this was an area worthy of diving into God and praying with the tenacity and fervency Mama exhibited. Maybe Kat could develop that closeness in a relationship of her own with God.

The thought excited her.

If that was the only reason she went through this with Jack, it was reason enough.

The final home game for the Blossoms had a bittersweet note to it. Even if they won, it wouldn't be enough to elevate them to the playoffs.

The season would end.

The locker room didn't ring with the banter and good-natured joshing that usually filled it before a game.

"All right, girls, gather round." Addebary gestured for them to circle around him. The players obeyed, some kneeling and others grabbing a bench. "It's been a good season. We're not heading where we'd hoped. But I want you to go out there and leave Cherry Hill with a game it won't forget. One they'll talk about all winter and that will draw the locals back to the very first game of the season.

"It's an honor to be your manager. I couldn't be prouder of another team. Let's play ball."

Joanie cleared her throat.

"Right. Let's pray first." Everyone whipped their caps off and bowed their heads. "God, thank You for the season and for each of the players. I ask You to keep them safe for one more game. Give them a good off-season with their families. And if it's not too much trouble, could we have one last win? For the fans? Amen.

"Now let's play ball."

Kat followed her teammates to the dugout. They formed the victory V one last time, and tears clouded her vision. She needed to go home, but she'd miss this. Would she be back? She didn't know. She couldn't focus on that question right now, or the tears would escape.

After a local school chorus sang "The "Star-Spangled

Banner" and the crowd recited the Pledge of Allegiance, it was time to play. The Blossoms batted in the bottom half of the inning. Kat sat on the bench, yelling encouragement to Annalise.

Annalise missed a ball right down the heart of the plate. "That's okay, Annalise. You can hit the next one."

Lola shook her head. "You'll always be a goody-two-shoes, won't you, kid?"

"Probably."

"I've never met anyone quite like you."

Kat grinned at her. "You'll miss me. Might as well admit it."

"Sad thing is, you're probably right."

The first five innings passed in a draw. Neither team could pull ahead. Instead the game turned into a pitchers' duel.

In the bottom of the ninth, Kat stood and made her way to the on-deck circle. She felt the pressure tighten her shoulders as she grabbed a bat and took a couple of practice swings. She wasn't a bad batter, hitting .264 over the season. She didn't like that the seventh-inning stretch came and went with the scoreboard showing zeros. Now in the ninth, time was running out.

Sweat trickled down her forehead and streamed down the small of her back. Lola swung hard but missed.

"Strike three. You're out." The umpire pumped his arm while Lola muttered and stomped back to the bench.

"Come on, Kat! Keep your eye on the ball, and swing for the fences!" Rosie's shout carried over the crowd noise.

"Sure thing." If only it were that easy: Tell her body what to do, and it'd happen.

"You can do it." Annalise's encouragement calmed the tremor shuddering through Kat.

Kat tried to imagine Jack in the stands, encouraging her to make it happen. He'd say she was a star and look at her like she had no choice but to hit a home run.

God, help me do my best.

She closed her eyes, took a deep breath, opened her eyes, and stepped up to the plate. A coolness settled over her. She'd found the place where all of life narrowed down to that small ball. The stands faded to a softened blend of color and noise. She could almost feel the pitcher's breathing.

The pitcher wound up and let loose a ball that sped toward the plate, but it sank low. Kat held her stance, not taking the bait.

"Ball!"

One down, three more to come.

The next pitch whizzed toward her ear. Kat spun in an attempt to avoid getting hit in the head again. She righted herself and turned to glare at the pitcher.

"Ball two! Two and O!"

"Come on, Kat." Rosie's voice carried from third base. "Just give me a shot. That's all I need."

Kat nodded, never taking her eyes off the pitcher. The next pitch seemed to bob and weave as it flew toward her. Kat stepped into it and swung with all her might. She thought she'd missed, when the top of the bat connected tipping the ball into the air. Rosie took off from third, head down, and barreled toward home. Kat hesitated a moment, trying to see if the ball was foul then took off down the baseline. Her legs pumped as she turned toward second. The crowd whooped and hollered. Kat reached second base and watched Rosie collide with the catcher and the ball roll from the catcher's hand.

Addebary raced to Rosie and spun her around.

Kat smiled. Finally Rosie had her chance to be the star. How fitting that it came in the final game of the season.

The Blossoms stormed from the dugout, surrounding Addebary and Rosie. Kat jogged the rest of the way around the bases, and Lola pulled her into the celebration. Soon Kat and Rosie bounced across the field on their teammates' shoulders.

The fans raced down and joined the party. They seemed eager to celebrate the win, even though the season had ended. The team went to Addebary's home to celebrate. Kat's teammates bubbled with plans for the rest of the year.

"I'll head back to Wisconsin and teach my first-grade class again." Annalise smiled as if she couldn't wait to get back to the room full of noisy six-year-olds. "There's nothing like watching their faces brighten when they understand addition or first read a book."

Rosie grimaced. "You can have the wee ones. I'll spend the year back at my dad's dairy. Doing the same things I've done every day since I learned to walk." Her face soured further. Guess the excitement of her starring role in the game had expired. "And each morning I'll count down to how many days are left before I come back."

"So you decided to come back to Cherry Hill after all?" Lola eyed Rosie over the top of her glass of tea.

"You bet. What else would I do?" Rosie nibbled a cherry.

Addebary caught Kat's eye and motioned toward his tiny kitchen. Kat stood and followed him into the room. "Have you reached a decision? I don't want to spend spring training looking for a new shortstop."

Kat stared at the tips of her shoes. "I'll need to talk to my parents when I get home."

"They let you come this year."

"True. I'm just not sure what next year holds."

Addebary crossed his arms and leaned against the counter. "What more do you need, kid? You know we want you back."

"I know. I guess I need to figure out what's after school."

"Sure. But all of that can include coming back next summer."

Kat laughed. "You are one persistent man."

"That I am—especially when the town fathers have ordered me to bring back our star player."

"You're kind, but others can do what I did."

"Not in a way that fills the stands."

"I'll keep praying about it." Kat slipped out of the room, hugged her teammates, and then headed home. She needed to pack, but first she needed to clear her head. Remove the confusion and lingering cobwebs from the season. Frankly she was so tired from the pace of the season and the thought of returning home and jumping straight into school that the idea of repeating the season drained her.

❧

Dayton didn't have the energy and excitement of downtown Chicago, but it certainly wasn't as sleepy as Cherry Hill. As Jack explored the city for the perfect apartment, he'd settled on a charming neighborhood blocks from downtown and near the National Cash Register Company. Near the University of Dayton, trees lined the sidewalks and the homes were old and substantial. He lived over another garage for another widow, but he liked the sense of independence, coupled with the role of protecting guardian.

The September morning had a chill to it as he headed toward the *Dayton Times*. The newsroom was bigger with more stringers running in and out, giving it a pulse that made the Cherry Hill paper look empty.

But then he had spent a summer covering girls' softball there.

Here his days and nights were filled with covering various government meetings, interspersed with teas and social events. Truly eclectic and very different from the sports page.

One thing he hadn't planned with the move was how to reconnect with Miss Katherine Miller. Thoughts of her haunted his days and lonely nights. He'd seen on the wire the Blossoms had won their final game. . .not enough to get them in the playoffs but enough to leave them feeling good. A positive springboard for next year.

What if Kat wanted to play again next year?

There were so many things he could worry about if he let

himself, but what was the point?

He could generate a list of experiences he and Kat needed to have before he spent too much energy on next year. But first, he had to find out if she was home. And if she had time to see him. Or was the life of a high school senior too intense to hang out with a geezer like him?

During his next break he grabbed the nearest phone and asked the operator to connect him to Kat's number.

"Hello?"

"Is this Mrs. Miller?"

"Yes?" The warmth in her voice didn't hide the question.

"This is Jack Raymond, a friend of Kat's. I wondered if she'd made it home yet from Cherry Hill."

"Yes, she's back and in school. Working hard to catch up on the days she missed."

"Good." Jack worried his lower lip.

"Can I take a message for her?"

"Just let her know Jack called."

"Oh, Jack. Are you the reporter she talks about?"

"Yes, if she says nice things about me."

The woman laughed. "Yes, she does. I remember meeting you in South Bend. Why don't you join us for dinner if you're in town?"

Jack quickly accepted, curious to know what Kat's expression would be when she saw him. He'd know a lot with that glance, though he wondered why she hadn't mentioned to her family that he'd moved to Dayton. After getting directions and realizing he lived in the neighborhood, Jack hung up, anticipation pumping through him.

In a matter of hours he'd see Kat again. Maybe she'd missed him as much as he'd missed her. A man could hope.

twenty

By four o'clock Kat wanted to catch the next train headed west. The day had passed slowly at school, but at least her friends seemed to have a new respect for her ball playing. Unknown to her at the time, the *Times* had run some of Jack's wire articles during the season.

Amazing what a difference an article could make.

Still, the thought of nine months filled with days that mirrored this one horrified her. The summer had spoiled her with its constant activity. It may have worn her out, but she'd felt alive. She wouldn't miss the strawberries sitting in classes, but her body already felt dormant, legs slack, arms useless.

It didn't take much effort to hold a pencil and scribble a couple of notes.

The final bell sounded, and Kat launched from her chair.

"See you tomorrow, Kat." Joanna, her constant companion last year, waved as she hurried out of the classroom. She stopped in the doorway. "You want to join some of us at the dime store for a Coke?"

"Can't. I'm supposed to help my sister with her kids tonight." Another change from when she left. It was odd not being the youngest in the house anymore. "See you next week." Kat stuffed her last assignment into her satchel and closed the flap. She walked to the door and collided with a solid chest. She looked up, up into Bobby Richardson's smoky eyes.

"Welcome back. I wondered if you'd decided to stay away."

"I agreed to come home before I signed the contract." Kat shrugged. It had certainly taken him long enough to track her down.

"Did you see the article the paper ran on you?" Was that

admiration in his eyes? "Jeepers, Kat. You made an impression on somebody. Being selected out of so many trying out."

"I guess."

Bobby starred on the high school baseball team, and their friendship had slowly developed last year. Then she would have done anything to have him look at her in such an assessing way. Now his eyes weren't the right color. She wanted someone else to show the interest in her.

"Can I walk you home?"

Kat cocked her head and considered him. "Isn't that out of your way?"

"It's not a problem. I'd like to hear about your season."

"All right." What could it hurt? Even if he wasn't the man she wanted to be with, he'd help the blocks pass.

During the walk, Bobby coaxed stories from her, until Kat wearied of talking and tried to turn the attention back to him. Finally they reached the walkway to her home. "See you Monday, Bobby."

He handed her bag over after a moment. "See ya." He saluted her and sauntered down the sidewalk as if he didn't have a care in the world. Kat watched a minute, empty from the assurance that boys like Bobby held no interest for her anymore.

No, a certain man had stolen her heart with his ability to see into her heart and coax her to believe in herself. Jack had known she could contribute in a real way to the Blossoms. His belief had transformed her.

Boys like Bobby couldn't compare. Not anymore.

Jack Raymond had ruined her.

Kat turned to her house, dreading a night filled with the noise and activity that had invaded with the return of Josie and her children. After her summer she needed some peace and quiet, but this wasn't the place to find it. She took a step up the sidewalk but stopped when she noticed a figure sitting in Mama's rocking chair.

And it wasn't Mama.

In that instant every stifled hope surged to life.

He'd come back.

Just like he'd said, Jack hadn't forgotten her.

The future was theirs, filled with the hope of a promise.

❧

A rumble of thunder sounded, one that matched the clanging in his head as Jack watched the kid saunter off. He wanted to read Kat's mind. She hadn't appeared engaged, keeping a couple of feet between her and that boy.

Maybe he should leave now. Before he did something crazy that revealed how insanely, over-the-moon, crazy-in-love with Kat he was. Especially since Kat stood on the sidewalk, white as a sheet, still as a statute, her gaze glued to him. She licked her lips but still didn't move. Guess he'd hoped for a different reaction. Anything more than this.

He pushed out of the rocker, sensing it whiz into motion behind him. He grabbed his fedora, slammed it on his head, and danced down the stairs. No way he'd let her see how her lack of emotion impacted him like a head to the chest in a brawl. He drew closer then stopped. Twin tears trailed down her cheeks.

Tears?

He hated tears. Didn't know how to respond to them. Always did and said the wrong thing. Why did women have to cry so much? And couldn't Kat provide a clue as to whether they were good or bad tears?

He took a hitched step forward. Stopped two feet from her. Kat's chin dipped as if she wanted to hide her tears. "Kat?"

She took a step forward and was in his arms before he could move. "Where have you been? Why did you leave before I did? Do you have any idea how lonely it was in Cherry Hill without you? And then you weren't here?" Her words blubbered on top of each other, and all Jack could do was circle her with his arms and put his chin on top of her head. She fit so well next to him.

How could he have thought of walking away a minute ago?

A throat cleared, and though Kat tried to step out of his embrace, he tightened his hold.

"Katherine Miller?" The tone was firm as it questioned.

Jack looked into her father's eyes. "Sir."

"I believe you have an introduction to make."

Kat settled against Jack's side. "Daddy, I hope you remember Jack Raymond from your trip to South Bend. Jack, this is my daddy."

"You can call me Louis." The man shook Jack's hand with an extra-firm grip. Message received. No one could hurt his baby girl without going through him. Jack respected that. "Darling, let's get Jack inside and reintroduce him to Mama."

"I've already met her. In fact, she's the one who invited me."

Kat's head bounced off his shoulder as she turned to look at him.

Jack studied her. "What?"

"Mama's intuition working overtime again."

Louis laughed. "You know better than that, Kat. I'd call it her prayer life."

"Yes, Daddy." Kat looked at Jack. "You've only got one more person to survive."

He quirked his eyebrows.

"My brother. He's a typical big brother. Loving. Picks on me. Overprotective."

"That worries me."

Kat grinned, the last shadow of tears clearing from her face. "He should." She looked Jack up and down. "He's bigger than you."

Jack puffed up at the challenge. "I can take him."

"I hope you don't have to." A wistful quality lengthened her words.

"Me, too, Kat. Me, too." Jack squared his shoulders and led her to the door.

Dinner was a loud affair, the table surrounded by Mr. and

Mrs. Miller; Kat's sister, Josie, and her kids; and Kat and Jack. Mark didn't make his appearance until dessert. The conversation bubbled around them, chaotic and scattered, while all Jack wanted to do was take Kat to the side and hear about how the season ended. Learn where her heart was now that she'd returned home.

After Kat helped clean up the supper dishes, her mother shooed them out the door. "Why don't you two walk a bit?"

"Don't be too long." Her daddy didn't even look up from his newspaper.

A soft smile brightened Kat's expression. "Guess you passed Daddy's inspection."

That was good. Now he wanted to pass hers. Kat grabbed a small bag that sat tucked in a corner of the porch. He reached for her hand as they strolled down the street, deeper into the neighborhood.

"Let's turn here." Kat led him around a corner.

"Why do I get the feeling you've got a plan?"

"Maybe I do. Don't worry. It's a spot we can catch up but also do something fun."

"Lead on." He grinned when she led him to an open field. Mature trees dotted it, but lines in the grass delineated a baseball diamond. He should have known she'd bring them to a spot where she could be completely comfortable. If she was, then he would be, too.

She opened her bag and pulled out two well-worn baseball gloves and a ball ready to come apart at the seams.

"Do you think the ball will last?"

"I'd be more concerned about the glove. It's Mark's." She winked at him over her shoulder as she sashayed away from him. She had no idea what she did to him. "Ready?" She whipped the ball his way before he had the glove on.

He sidestepped out of the way, and Kat laughed while he pulled the glove on and crab walked to the ball. "This is why I cover sports."

Kat sobered instantly. "Do you regret it?"

"Regret what?" He had to hear her answer.

She plopped down on the grass, her skirt billowing around her. "Moving here. For me."

"Katherine Miller, I could never regret that. You are the most amazing woman I've ever known. And I knew I didn't want to stay in Cherry Hill. Dayton's a good move."

"But what if I go back to Cherry Hill next summer?"

There. That was the crux of the issue. "Addebary still trying to get you to commit?"

She nodded, chin wobbling. He sat down next to her, leaned over, and kissed her before she could succumb to more tears. She clung to him, returning his kiss. He pulled back, staring into her eyes. "Are you listening to me, Kat?" She nodded, but he couldn't tell if she really heard. "You need to get this, though I'll say it as often as you need. I want to be with you. You're the woman I want to forge my future with. If that means we return to Cherry Hill from time to time, I'll go gladly as long as you're with me."

"Do you mean that?"

"Absolutely."

"Good." She smiled at him in a way that made him sit back, wondering what was coming. "Because you've spoiled me for all the high school boys. And everyone else is off fighting." She tried to slip away, but he wouldn't let go.

"I think that comment entitles me to another kiss."

A sweet smile lit her face from the inside. As the ball and glove dropped to the ground, Jack leaned closer. And in that moment, he sensed the power of a future forged on a promise of forever.

Letter to Readers

I hope you enjoyed reading Kat and Jack's story. I had a great time watching it unfold. There was something fun about Kat—her spunk made this book a joy to write.

The All-American Girls Professional Softball League was a very real experiment that began the summer of 1943 and continued until 1954. The first summer, there were only four teams. I created Cherry Hill, Indiana, and the Cherry Hill Blossoms because, despite the excellent help of Scott Shuler, archivist at the Center for History in South Bend, Indiana, which houses the archives of the AAGPS/BL, I was unable to find the exact dates and play schedules of the 1943 season. Rather than create too much havoc with real events, I created two shadow teams. How the teams traveled, the rules, the uniforms and other details are all accurate reflections. Just don't look for Cherry Hill, the Cherry Hill Blossoms, or the Joliet Jewels.

Though you might not be a baseball fan, I hope you enjoyed Kat's story of learning to be a light for Christ and to stand on her own faith—important lessons for all of us.

It's always a joy to write for you!
Cara

A Letter To Our Readers

Dear Reader:
In order that we might better contribute to your reading enjoyment, we would appreciate your taking a few minutes to respond to the following questions. We welcome your comments and read each form and letter we receive. When completed, please return to the following:

Fiction Editor
Heartsong Presents
PO Box 719
Uhrichsville, Ohio 44683

1. Did you enjoy reading *A Promise Forged* by Cara C. Putman?
   ❑ Very much! I would like to see more books by this author!
   ❑ Moderately. I would have enjoyed it more if
   ____
   ____
   ____

2. Are you a member of **Heartsong Presents**? ❑ Yes ❑ No
   If no, where did you purchase this book? ________________
   ____

3. How would you rate, on a scale from 1 (poor) to 5 (superior), the cover design? ____________________________

4. On a scale from 1 (poor) to 10 (superior), please rate the following elements.

____ Heroine	____ Plot
____ Hero	____ Inspirational theme
____ Setting	____ Secondary characters

5. These characters were special because? ________________

____

____

6. How has this book inspired your life? ________________

____

____

7. What settings would you like to see covered in future **Heartsong Presents** books? ________________________

____

____

8. What are some inspirational themes you would like to see treated in future books? ________________________

____

____

9. Would you be interested in reading other **Heartsong Presents** titles? ❑ Yes ❑ No

10. Please check your age range:

❑ Under 18 ❑ 18-24
❑ 25-34 ❑ 35-45
❑ 46-55 ❑ Over 55

Name ____

Occupation ___________________________________

Address ______________________________________

City, State, Zip ________________________________

E-mail _______________________________________

Heartsong

Any 12
Heartsong
Presents titles
for only
$27.00*

HISTORICAL ROMANCE IS CHEAPER BY THE DOZEN!

Buy any assortment of twelve *Heartsong Presents* titles and save 25% off of the already discounted price of $2.97 each!

*plus $4.00 shipping and handling per order and sales tax where applicable. If outside the U.S. please call 740-922-7280 for shipping charges.

HEARTSONG PRESENTS TITLES AVAILABLE NOW:

__HP663 *Journeys*, T. H. Murray
__HP664 *Chance Adventure*, K. E. Hake
__HP667 *Sagebrush Christmas*, B. L. Etchison
__HP668 *Duel Love*, B. Youree
__HP671 *Sooner or Later*, V. McDonough
__HP672 *Chance of a Lifetime*, K. E. Hake
__HP675 *Bayou Secrets*, K. M. Y'Barbo
__HP676 *Beside Still Waters*, T. V. Bateman
__HP679 *Rose Kelly*, J. Spaeth
__HP680 *Rebecca's Heart*, L. Harris
__HP683 *A Gentlemen's Kiss*, K. Comeaux
__HP684 *Copper Sunrise*, C. Cox
__HP687 *The Ruse*, T. H. Murray
__HP688 *A Handful of Flowers*, C. M. Hake
__HP691 *Bayou Dreams*, K. M. Y'Barbo
__HP692 *The Oregon Escort*, S. P. Davis
__HP695 *Into the Deep*, L. Bliss
__HP696 *Bridal Veil*, C. M. Hake
__HP699 *Bittersweet Remembrance*, G. Fields
__HP700 *Where the River Flows*, I. Brand
__HP703 *Moving the Mountain*, Y. Lehman
__HP704 *No Buttons or Beaux*, C. M. Hake
__HP707 *Mariah's Hope*, M. J. Conner
__HP708 *The Prisoner's Wife*, S. P. Davis
__HP711 *A Gentle Fragrance*, P. Griffin
__HP712 *Spoke of Love*, C. M. Hake
__HP715 *Vera's Turn for Love*, T. H. Murray
__HP716 *Spinning Out of Control*, V. McDonough
__HP719 *Weaving a Future*, S. P. Davis
__HP720 *Bridge Across the Sea*, P. Griffin
__HP723 *Adam's Bride*, L. Harris
__HP724 *A Daughter's Quest*, L. N. Dooley
__HP727 *Wyoming Hoofbeats*, S. P. Davis
__HP728 *A Place of Her Own*, L. A. Coleman
__HP731 *The Bounty Hunter and the Bride*, V. McDonough
__HP732 *Lonely in Longtree*, J. Stengl
__HP735 *Deborah*, M. Colvin
__HP736 *A Time to Plant*, K. E. Hake
__HP740 *The Castaway's Bride*, S. P. Davis
__HP741 *Golden Dawn*, C. M. Hake
__HP743 *Broken Bow*, I. Brand
__HP744 *Golden Days*, M. Connealy
__HP747 *A Wealth Beyond Riches*, V. McDonough
__HP748 *Golden Twilight*, K. Y'Barbo
__HP751 *The Music of Home*, T. H. Murray
__HP752 *Tara's Gold*, L. Harris
__HP755 *Journey to Love*, L. Bliss
__HP756 *The Lumberjack's Lady*, S. P. Davis
__HP759 *Stirring Up Romance*, J. L. Barton
__HP760 *Mountains Stand Strong*, I. Brand
__HP763 *A Time to Keep*, K. E. Hake
__HP764 *To Trust an Outlaw*, R. Gibson
__HP767 *A Bride Idea*, Y. Lehman
__HP768 *Sharon Takes a Hand*, R. Dow
__HP771 *Canteen Dreams*, C. Putman
__HP772 *Corduroy Road to Love*, L. A. Coleman
__HP775 *Treasure in the Hills*, P. W. Dooly
__HP776 *Betsy's Return*, W. E. Brunstetter
__HP779 *Joanna's Adventure*, M. J. Conner
__HP780 *The Dreams of Hannah Williams*, L. Ford
__HP783 *Seneca Shadows*, L. Bliss
__HP784 *Promises, Promises*, A. Miller
__HP787 *A Time to Laugh*, K. Hake
__HP788 *Uncertain Alliance*, M. Davis
__HP791 *Better Than Gold*, L. A. Eakes
__HP792 *Sweet Forever*, R. Cecil

(If ordering from this page, please remember to include it with the order form.)

Presents

__HP795 *A Treasure Reborn,* P. Griffin
__HP796 *The Captain's Wife,* M. Davis
__HP799 *Sandhill Dreams,* C. C. Putman
__HP800 *Return to Love,* S. P. Davis
__HP803 *Quills and Promises,* A. Miller
__HP804 *Reckless Rogue,* M. Davis
__HP807 *The Greatest Find,* P. W. Dooly
__HP808 *The Long Road Home,* R. Druten
__HP811 *A New Joy,* S.P. Davis
__HP812 *Everlasting Promise,* R.K. Cecil
__HP815 *A Treasure Regained,* P. Griffin
__HP816 *Wild at Heart,* V. McDonough
__HP819 *Captive Dreams,* C. C. Putman
__HP820 *Carousel Dreams,* P. W. Dooly
__HP823 *Deceptive Promises,* A. Miller
__HP824 *Alias, Mary Smith,* R. Druten
__HP827 *Abiding Peace,* S. P. Davis
__HP828 *A Season for Grace,* T. Bateman
__HP831 *Outlaw Heart,* V. McDonough
__HP832 *Charity's Heart,* R. K. Cecil
__HP835 *A Treasure Revealed,* P. Griffin
__HP836 *A Love for Keeps,* J. L. Barton
__HP839 *Out of the Ashes,* R. Druten
__HP840 *The Petticoat Doctor,* P. W. Dooly
__HP843 *Copper and Candles,* A. Stockton
__HP844 *Aloha Love,* Y. Lehman
__HP847 *A Girl Like That,* F. Devine
__HP848 *Remembrance,* J. Spaeth
__HP851 *Straight for the Heart,* V. McDonough
__HP852 *A Love All Her Own,* J. L. Barton
__HP855 *Beacon of Love,* D. Franklin
__HP856 *A Promise Kept,* C. C. Putman
__HP859 *The Master's Match,* T. H. Murray
__HP860 *Under the Tulip Poplar,* D. Ashley & A. McCarver
__HP863 *All that Glitters,* L. Sowell
__HP864 *Picture Bride,* Y. Lehman
__HP867 *Hearts and Harvest,* A. Stockton
__HP868 *A Love to Cherish,* J. L. Barton
__HP871 *Once a Thief,* F. Devine
__HP872 *Kind-Hearted Woman,* J. Spaeth
__HP875 *The Bartered Bride,* E. Vetsch
__HP876 *A Promise Born,* C.C. Putman
__HP877 *A Still, Small Voice,* K. O'Brien
__HP878 *Opie's Challenge,* T. Fowler
__HP879 *A Bouquet for Iris,* D. Ashley & A. McCarver
__HP880 *The Glassblower,* L.A. Eakes
__HP883 *Patterns and Progress,* A. Stockton
__HP884 *Love From Ashes,* Y. Lehman
__HP887 *The Marriage Masquerade,* E. Vetsch
__HP888 *In Search of a Memory,* P. Griffin
__HP891 *Sugar and Spice,* F. Devine
__HP892 *The Mockingbird's Call,* D. Ashley and A. McCarver

Great Inspirational Romance at a Great Price!

Heartsong Presents books are inspirational romances in contemporary and historical settings, designed to give you an enjoyable, spirit-lifting reading experience. You can choose wonderfully written titles from some of today's best authors like Wanda E. Brunstetter, Mary Connealy, Susan Page Davis, Cathy Marie Hake, Joyce Livingston, and many others.

When ordering quantities less than twelve, above titles are $2.97 each.
Not all titles may be available at time of order.

SEND TO: **Heartsong Presents** Readers' Service
P.O. Box 721, Uhrichsville, Ohio 44683
Please send me the items checked above. I am enclosing $ ______
(please add $4.00 to cover postage per order. OH add 7% tax. WA add 8.5%). Send check or money order, no cash or C.O.D.s, please.
To place a credit card order, call 1-740-922-7280.

NAME ______________________________

ADDRESS ______________________________

CITY/STATE ____________________ ZIP ________

HPS 4-10